Vampire`s Bur

Written by Tanya Coleby © 2024.

Cover art by Karen at Storygraphixplus

Letter work by Tanya Coleby.

misstcoleby2@gmail.com

Tanya Coleby author on - FB, Tik Tok, Twitter x and Instagram.

If you can, please could review it afterwards, I would appreciate it so much.

Take care x

An m/m Invisible Vampire spin-off.

This series of events occurs after his Invisible Hate book two, but it can be read as a two-part stand-alone.

In this series, Vampire`s live high up in the vampire realm and take souls to their final destination. They can only be seen by other immortals and their one human-fated mate.

VAMPIRE'S
BURNING
DESIRE

CHAPTER ONE

Then

Deacon

Putting his stuff together in a hurry back down into the
favourite of his overflowing orange, Nike sports bag in the
men's changing rooms, Deacon took a large thirst-quenching
swig out of his extremely cool and refreshing water bottle
and got ready to leave the gym at long last after a tiring work
out that had now dulled his senses.

His ass was beyond numb.

Everything hurt him all over so darn bad and his muscles
ached. Needing rest. From standing up on his feet all day at
work and walking around, and now finishing a satisfying but
tiring workout in the late evening.

Licking the drops of water slowly away that were oozing out
of his mouth with a long lingering searching tongue.

Enjoying the liquid dripping down his throat. Quenching his thirst for a time.

But not his soul.

That in itself was empty. He did not know why, but it was. Something was missing in his life.

Or maybe… someone…

He started to walk off now that he was all set to leave the packed gym behind and so hesitantly walked off towards the nearest exit in long strides with a new shade of confidence in his step. A smile upon his face.

Feeling like his body was taking shape into the look that he so wanted it to be after long last.

No longer the fat, spotty, bullied kid that he had been whilst back at school, he had worked hard to get out of that, and he would never let himself feel that way again.

Feeling hopeless.

Feeling strangely good about himself now back in the present, he had a feeling inside that the evening was about to get so much better, but he did not quite know why…

Casting a parting glance behind him now nervously with a hidden crimson blush on his cheeks, hanging near to the vending machines, ones that Deacon would certainly not use even if you paid him to, given as he only ate healthy the majority of the time now since becoming an adult, and there was not an iota of healthy food in those machines from what he could now see!

Still.

A stupid idea to have in a gym if you asked him!

Give him a salad or plain meat any day of the week. It might not taste that good, but it kept his muscles and weight just the way that he liked them.

And any admirers also.

Not that there were too many of them knocking at his door as of recently…it had been a dry spell in the bed sheets that was for sure.

As he slowly turned his auburn-haired head to the side he then to his excitement caught a cheeky wink off of his current crush – Stevie Jay, who was now staring his way silently brooding whilst leaning against the tempting Mars machine, as if he thought that it was Deacon, that was made from head to toe of pure sinful chocolate instead of the tempting goods inside it.

Ok, maybe he had one admirer then that he could name…

It could be arranged, Deacon thought with a sudden warm buzzing glow as the other guy took him in like temptation itself.

Well, he would not mind it one bit if the other bigger, tattooed guy gradually picked him out with his long slender fingers and then ate him up from head to toe, although Deacon added in his mind that he would have to purchase said chocolate in order to drench himself in it, watching and waiting as he was slowly nibbled, licked, sucked - starting with a certain massive…

Thoughts abruptly left his mind as Stevie boldly came towards Deacon in his faithful grey three-striped tracksuit almost flying over in his eagerness to get there it seemed, donning the grey one that showed every inch of his toned, sculpted figure off, especially his fine rounded ass, and so it also stopped the auburn one right there in his tracks, in the centre of the packed gym.

Hesitant. Cautious.

Caught like a deer in headlights out of his comfort zone. A dog with its tongue out waiting for a treat. Either one of those it could be.

The other more confident man went on to say, "Hey, catch ya next time, little Deacon boy," Stevie smirked this with a naughty glint in his brown eyes that lit up with warmth on seeing him again.

An intense gaze that soon brought Deacon out of his fucked-up dirty gym fantasies and casually salivating at a man who was much bigger than he was.

Taller. Packed.

Which wasn't hard.

Little, what a cheek! He would show him little if he wanted! Deacon knew that he had to stop coming there to this gym in the city near his place of work, as he silently cursed at his extended embarrassment by his dishy, tattooed suitor! Knowing that it was no good for him to do this dick-wielding dance that they did so every week without fail.

Flirting, but yet nothing after that except a fond goodbye and a fare well, tara!

He was no good for him he really wasn't. The chocolate there that made one's yearning mouth water was no good for him either and Stevie and them both combined – not so good.

Deacon needed for his own sanity to stay healthy, as healthy as he could possibly be, and so he could be slightly muscular at all angles, and he didn't want to be there at the gym only to gawp at the passing eye candy when it could put him off his stride.

Make him weak. Weaker.

Make him what he used to be when he still lived under his parent's roof. And at school. An everyday nightmare.

A victim. And he wasn't that. Not anymore.

Never again.

Pure and pure eye candy – and Stevie J knew it with a vengeance as he turned heads wherever he went. Whenever he went.

He blatantly loved it how the girls, the men, and even the staff, everyone on the way - side-eyed him. Taking a sneaky peak.

He would admit it if probed. Although he and Stevie didn't have that advanced friendship quite as of yet, it was heading towards it after getting to know each other gradually over time.

But there was no personality there in the much bigger man's mischievous soul to speak of from what Deacon could tell of him that made him want to spend some more time with him. To date him.

He reckoned that there would be more personality there in the tall, towering, greenish-brown plant pot right near to the receptionist's desk than in his passing crush.

He could guarantee it.

But he found that he didn't mind this that much though and he knew that there was no chance of lasting romance between the two of them.

The dark-haired, bigger rascal had other traits that the tempted Deacon wanted to firmly get a hold of for a time with his firm grip, which would most certainly make up for it… almost drooling at the thought of it as his eyes tried not to linger at the showing tats as Stevie stretched out with a teasing grin.

Knowing what he was doing.

See this was the thing when you hadn't had any in a while, it was all you could think about day after day…night after night.

He was almost drooling at his scrumptious, posing new friend, not quite much else, there in his salivating lust.

Although the dark-haired male was not his usual type of fling to have – that was reserved for blondes, dirty blondes – the dirtier the better, them and them alone.

He didn't know what it was about them that took his fancy, but – they brought him to his knees where he liked to stay for them.

To be submissive. That was his thing.

It was such a shame that no one fitting that description had come into his path as of late…

Back in the gym, he shivered in desire which he hoped would be mistaken to as from the bare freezing cold as the heaters seemed to have packed in, and his potential target let out a slight laugh at his sheer blatant nervousness.

Lips smirking and eyes daring him to respond somehow.

Had he clocked him?

How he thought had Stevie even known that he was even gay just like he was?

Or did he not even care either way, if he wasn`t? Some men liked a challenge.

He was a challenge.

Deacon kept his personal life mainly to himself apart from revealing his status to those closest to him, dearest to him, whom he had decided that he most trusted in the world to keep it to themselves.

Not to gossip about it.

Not to hate him just like they had done at school back then.

Not that Stevie himself acted that way with his big, but perfect figure and daring look. Oozing confidence.

Deacon doubted that he had ever been bullied.

The other male was what was known as - an open book. He obviously didn't care who knew that he only liked men and enjoyed watching the women's faces fall when he turned them down flat with disinterest.

Because in their eyes, Stevie should like them back whether he wanted to or not.

Some people were certainly entitled.

Maybe Deacon wondered whether he should be more like that.

Confident. Uncaring.

But from his own raging father having found out his secret sexual preferences and only after breaking his son's trust and then reading his badly hidden diary, finding his questionable porn stash, and punching and beating him raw, chucking his only child out onto the streets just for wanting another that he felt that he shouldn`t do, with his heart broken and his few bags hastily packed together.

Standing there back then as a teen scared witless and flat out broke, stunned, with only his minimal stuff onto the lonely streets, had paid wind to that. After that, Deacon knew that he would never trust a man in his lifetime again.

Could never trust one.

Dared not to.

He feared it. His heart still held the lasting endless scars that his dad had left on it.

And there they would remain.

Even an attractive one spelt danger. Especially an attractive one…they were the worst ones to play with your mind.

Preferring to instead keep them all at arm's length from him and his heart intact in the process.

It was best that way.

It was the only way! For it must be!

But enough of that.

Deacon had announced that he would not let one certain fucked-up father put a dampener on things for him now if he could. Ten awesome years later was when life was now reasonably becoming good.

Sadly, his own mother hadn't left her husband after said beating and eviction of him, although she had helped him find a place to live, and so hence the twos mother/son relationship ever since had been what you would call stifled, but even through that life was still relatively good.

Sort of.

Given the circumstances anyway.

Wasn't it? From having it bad at school to losing all the family that you had cared about – it made you brave. It made you wary.

"Maybe, I will." Deacon shrugged carelessly in answer to spectacular Stevie and then stopped and waited for an answer back in return. Acting as if inside he was playing it cool with him when really he was quaking in his boots at the thought of rejection.

And possibly, ok quite obviously - erect. Deacon had caught the other walking around earlier topless with his perfection out in all its glory, and had felt hot and sweaty ever since, which he guessed was its desired effect. Stevie knew exactly what he was doing.

He smirked again more openly at Deacon and his gawping. Looking him again up and down whilst taking a bite of a KitKat - carefree.

Deacon wished that he was said Kit Kat, "You better have." He grinned.

Ok, he was now out of there before the tempting Stevie J, blew his secret cover and unveiled Deacon's sexuality that he tried to keep so desperately on the down low - to the rest of the world.

Throbbing fantasies over the equipment were delayed.

Deacon would not turn down women and tell them the truth of the matter, so instead he usually muddled along and made something up about why they couldn't date. Didn't want to reveal it to anyone who could use it against him.

Couldn't. It brought him out in a sweat.

"Drink?" A flirtatious glance from Stevie.

Should he?

He sighed and scuffed his trainers nervously together.

No.

Even though he was tempted to follow the bigger man to his car in the nearby car park like a sappy puppy, something stopped him. If he did this then he would be missing out on something else.

Something more. Better. It was there within in his reach.

He did not know what, but it was calling his name!

"No worries, little D." Stevie smiled with disappointment.

"Ok. See ya then." Ignoring the awkward silence.

Deacon threw the tipping bag over muscled aching shoulders and left through the main door of the building without delay.

But not before shouting out, "But less of the little yeah, hey?"

For he was not little in any way. That he would never be. Or want to be. Certainly not the biggest of men, no, but also certainly not the smallest of them either.

Not waiting for an answer from the other bloke with the bulshy guts and now blatantly ignoring the gym-going others looking at the two talking two and fro with hopefully hidden heat entwined, he then hurriedly left for home.

Feeling so out of his comfort zone right about then.

"You are little to me. Bye, Deacon!" Stevie winked cheekily his way. A wink meant for he and he alone.

He blushed. "Bye."

"I will text you. Hey?"

"Ok." Short and sweet, to the point. Still not little. He hated that!

The gym was the doubtful Deacon`s, go-to place where he went to after work at his stressful though enjoyable job as a veterinary nurse, soon to be qualified vet, at the nearby veterinary practice.

Most people he guessed were surprised to see a male nurse even working there when they first worryingly walked in for their loving pets' appointment and most deduced that the vets would be men and the nurses solely female just as they did in a human hospital.

But, he loved his job regardless of this notion. He had trained so hard for it all and had worked with animals since leaving school behind for good. There would be no other job for him given that he much preferred animals over mere people. They were too much hard work and animals were – everything to him.

Even if he got bitten, pecked, screamed at, weed on. He forgave them every single time that they did so.

He always would.

The cool air as he left hit the frazzled worked-out man, walking casually out of the smart well-painted building, and thus pulled his jacket tighter to his cooling, aching body. Even the exercise, the sweat couldn't warm him up on an evening just like this one. One where your toes went numb and your balls froze, shrivelled up and found somewhere warm, to hide.

He passed the city centre lined with tall, inviting shops enjoying the brisk walk home and the quietness that it brought him, the peace that he felt at the edge of his core that the workout had released in him somewhat, but then…

"Get off me!"

What the heck was happening?

What the heck was that? Interrupting him in his quiet zone.

His state of peace.

His heart thundered at a million beats a minute until it nearly left his chest behind for good.

Thud thud, thud thud.

Deacon heard it - clear as day through the cool, before then calm night that surrounded him. It seemed to be to him as he listened nervously – the panicked sound of a sweet woman's voice coming from nearby down one of the back roads, but there.

A woman in distress.

A damsel! Hmm… he didn't know how he felt about that one.

Then to his despair as he gritted his teeth and eyes glued to the other side of the road in alarm - the sound of screaming, shouting, clawing, whatnot, added to the unease that he was already beginning to feel in the pit of his stomach.

A flat stomach – a hungry stomach now filled with upcoming dread at the startling sounds that were coming from someplace right there near him.

Something was not right down there - he knew that. Heck, anyone in hearing distance would know that.

Something was – off you might be inclined to say …

Oh, it was coming from an alleyway he realised with a jolt as he spun round to trace the sound of the panicked woman's screams! An unnerving chill crept down his spine as he thought with dread about what could be happening down there in the dark, from which he could not see.

Not liking the sound of it at all, hating conflict in any way, shape, or form, but even so, he would stand up for what was right even - if he got caught there in the crossfire and met his doom in a hate-filled world.

He was a good guy really.

Attracted to bad ones though -this had been his specialty.

Cos who doesn't love a villain rather than a simping hero?

Few would admit it – he would.

Deacon would hold his hands up and admit that he had always been attracted to the villains in the movies. Wanting to be taken, chained, and dominated by them.

Though not poison ivy or Harley Quinn. He preferred a bit of Spike, Eric – James even. He had beaten off to James quite a few times after watching him in a certain vampire, teen saga. Though he was not sure he liked the whole idea of dating a rampant, blonde vampire, he could fantasise about the idea of being fucked by one with a alcoholic drink in one hand and his cock in the other!

A bottom through and through.

Deacon anxiously turned his head down the long, eerie street and realised numbly that there was no one that he could see in his near sight, no one around to help that poor, poor screaming, terrified presumably woman - but him.

If this went down the pan here and now then he was sadly all alone with his misery.

That that day may be his last gym; eye-candy workout. Tomorrow - he may done for. On the news as a predator's heroic victim. Gone without a trace.

He knew now that he should have gotten a lift from Stevie when asked, he just knew it! But he or they both knew where that would have ended up. Unclothed and in bed frolicking together, rolling around hot and sweaty, caressing, thrusting, possibly chocolate covered and groaning wildly, when what he truly needed was an early night to be up and ready for work tomorrow in one piece.

And not to complicate things. Their friendship.

The punishing days patting pets and dodging scary-ass pet owners and occasional evenings and weekends doing overtime - they took it out of you.

You became – boring.

Feeling old.

Deacon finally approached the eerie alleyway cautiously with a jagged house key that he had taken from his bag in his hand for good measure. Knowing that it might not kill anyone off if he aimed it their way, wouldn't do a lot of damage, but it could help him bide some time if he needed it.

Also having a sudden brain wave he pulled the heavy bag off of his bulky curved shoulders also, just in case he needed to hit someone so bloody hard with it to knock them out. Take the wind out of their sails.

He might have some muscles on him – sure, but he had flopped at self-defence classes in every way that was possible to flop at. Been put on his ass.

More than once. With no happy ending.

Yes, as he listened cautiously he then heard it again more loudly this time as if it was there in his echoing mind in the quiet for a change city street. A woman's shrieking voice pleading with someone to leave her the heck alone, or else she would scream a loud.

Kick them in the nuts.

It must be bad, he gasped with one hand on his beating chest. The other one still clutching the key awkwardly with a shake. He was not afraid to use it!

She sounded frantic from what Deacon could tell with her pained words and horrible girly screaming. It was upsetting to hear; how could someone do that to another human he wondered...?

Some people sickened him. They really did. They already had. And this person responsible whoever they were certainly did the most.

It did not feel good either way to hear it either. It brought back unwanted memories that he would rather have stayed dead and buried of a time when he himself had been beaten and left in the dark by another stronger than he...

He had to be brave here, he knew it, but it addled him anyway.

He changed direction, heading for the cause of the woman's anguish.

He could just about see two figures, "Hey, what is going on?" Deacon asked now on approach down the shadowy, gloomy alley with only one light that flickered in the gloom and likely doom. One that needed a new bulb perhaps, some maintenance as it sparked when he neared it. If he had had a torch he would have whipped it out in a flash.

Used it as a weapon if it was needed.

But he did not. Note to self he thought to himself – purchase a new torch in case of emergencies such as this one, so that he could see or swing for someone, but one could not expect to need it on the short walk home through a crowded city that was usually friendly, frantic and fanbloodytastic!

An alleyway though that smelt remarkably like pure undiluted piss and fallen rotten garbage that proudly oozed out of the nearby bins. Ones that had not been emptied in an age it so seemed.

But, instead of a woman there in the alley in distress, unclothed or being attacked by a scummy, handsy bastard who couldn't obviously understand the word no, and been taken advantage of, maybe mugged, then there was only him…

One man there.

If that was what he was…because he was so bloody perfect that Deacon could not turn his gaze away from him. He was in complete and utter awe. His awe was in awe.

Everything was in awe! He stifled a groan as his hands shook and he put away the key. Shaking not necessarily from fear, more like from the sexual charge that lit up every nerve in his body, making him want to weep aloud.

Which was frankly stupid.

But it was where he was at right there as their interested gazes locked with each other. One man glued to the other and vice versa.

It was to be like entering hell and finding an angel situated there instead of the devil himself.

Perfection just like that did not deserve to be in this rotten place, in this rotten dump, in this particular alley. In this fine city that he had grown up in and had come to love.

And Deacon liked perfection, he strived for it in every way possible. At work, the gym and at play. The way he looked. And he wanted to play with this man here. Oh, yes he certainly did!

Perfection… this man was it with knobs on! Everything about him was just so perfect. The right size. The right height. Not an ounce of fat that the eye could see… if there was he would not care!

A face so chiselled that it could have been carved from god himself with perfection spare. Hair that hung slightly, but was not too long.

Deacon on seeing the drool-worthy male right there in his first line of sight let out an unmanly shuddering gasp and then flung a hand over his gawping mouth at the sight that lay there before him. Hadn't he have expected to see a

24

monster there deep in the alley? Hoping not anyway, but now he saw only something so divine, that he thought it was not possible that he was actually seeing it there in the sweet city of Norwich.

Sinful, surprising.

Sure.

Words could not ever be enough to explain just what he felt at that moment in time there in the creepy ass alley, all alone, but for one spectacular man. For some reason that he did not know of his heart uncharacteristically leapt in defiance before he had even seen him right there up close.

Butterflies danced in his belly.

Wanting to escape, wanting for him to get to know this man. The smell of the enticing stranger, only a scent of one of perfection, everything was, it took his breath away.

Completely.

It covered the searing sour miserable smell that lingered there along with the rubbish, until he could only erupt at the brilliance of it

The perfect stranger indeed. The perfect man – the perfect everything, just as Deacon liked it.

Wanted it. He oozed it.

One who made gym Stevie, look like a mere houseless tramp who would normally likely frequent this said alleyway begging for money, whilst chugging cheap cider out of the bottle by the litre.

Nothing and nobody that he had seen before in all of his twenty-eight years could yet amaze him in the same way that this flustered handsome god before him, with the luscious shaggy blonde hair, that fell just slightly over his stunning eerie eyes, this flustered from being there in an alley.

Puzzled now, "Where is the woman?" Deacon dared to ask the flummoxed man.

"Sorry? What woman? Oh, is he looking at me? You. No, you!" The blonde stuttered through his stunned thick lips, seeming confused. With a hint of stubble around them. His words echoed in the night.

Deacon's heart thumped again. Deacon then watched the blonde bombshell bite his lips nervously and a strange shot of red lit up his already beautiful yellowy, brown eyes, tinging them, they went the colour of pure scarlet.

Like a monster.

Deacon now knew that he should be scared as he took in the change in what humans eyes looked like that. Red tinged in warning.

Red-tinged in need.

None. None indeed and that was the truth of it.

But instead, he was simply – in fucking awe of the man whom he had just met because there would be no forgetting ever meeting someone like him. If he had, he would have eternally been on his mind.

In his heart and his bed.

Anchored to the ground the gym-worn Deacon couldn't run away even if he wanted to.

His soul put paid to that. It had met its match.

Likely his cock too. That was now rising like a boa constrictor looking for its next delicious meal. He could feel it dripping with need for its new daddy. Throbbing.

Wow. Dynamite.

Deacon thought it was like something out of a movie. He loved movies and books… not so much. A movie where instead of them bumping cheerily into each other at the supermarket buying meals for one, it was first coming across each other in a forbidden dark and lonely place.

An alley.

One that he never wanted to venture into again but would do if he saw the same beautiful sight lurking there in the shadows.

The blonde stranger then appeared to push something in front of him in a fluster and grab onto thin air as if he were trying to grab hold of something that was unseen, but except for him. Something that Deacon could only hear - words, but not yet see.

What was it he wondered? He glanced but remained still unsure. It sounded like a woman whispering right there in the dark, but there remained no one there, but the two males. The guy was up to something.

And Deacon was not Sherlock Holmes, but he would find out what it was.

Besides - he needed to know. Beginning to think that maybe he should have minded his own business and simply taken his tired self-off home…

But he was in far too deep now to back out.

Cursed his luck. Cursed this beautiful man before him. The one like an angel, the one like a sinner.

But what part?

With red-tinged eyes and a smirk like the guy wanted to eat him.

"What do you have there?" Deacon asked the godly man curiously, pointing whilst leaning to be on his tiptoe, peering his auburn head to catch a view of what was irking him and of him.

The heartthrob should come with, but a simple warning label.

Deacon's words caught in his throat.

For even in his heavily agitated, flustered state, his pale, pale skin like chalk, the messy hair that on another would have looked like it needed a good brush through, the blonde silent, the possibly violent creature was – simply to Deacon, to be almighty fine.

And that was putting it mildly.

There was a strange magnetic pull that drew him right in like a large magnet, a pull that kept him there, moulded to the ground. He knew that he should go, turn, and run now as fast as his trim legs could carry him back to his own, that he had likely imagined the woman for she was not there when she should be, even though he had for sure heard her, but he found that – he couldn't leave even if he wanted to.

Work feet, work, he cursed to himself!

But nope, they did not comply with him. Sneakers staying put on the ground. Rooted to the spot and perhaps even liking it there. Almost as if he was chained to the spot and held down into place with invisible chains.

A flush crept over Deacon's now cold face at the thought of it. That was hot.

The guy a dominating daddy. He would make a fine one! Deacon said with bite, "What have you done to me? Why can I not move from here? Who the hell are you? Oi, I am talking to you!" He stuttered this in complete and utter outrage at the strange situation that prevented him from moving from the spot where he was now currently frozen in place. Appearing to blame the stranger guy for the fact that he was stuck with him in that dark, deserted alley, alone together, rather cosy!

When the fact could simply be just because – he wanted to be there.

"He is talking to you."

Oh, he spoke now! A luscious bundle of words. Throaty, he would make a good narrator with a voice like that!

The unusual man muttered as if he was standing there solely with another, but the two of them.

Speaking to himself rather than straight to Deacon, who wished to god that he would speak to him and him only. Deacon found he liked hearing the words that left the marvellous full-lipped mouth.

He could listen to that gravelly voice that came from simply kissable lips, that made him want to weep all day if he let him. Lips that would suit being perched around the end of his thick cock, sucking all his cum messily, that dribbled from them.

Ok, poured... he would if he had a hottie like that at the end of it! Keeping going until they almost choked on what they had made him do.

But a guy like this, blonde and god-like, that was far too darn perfect in every way to be made to go down onto his bare knees in the grub of the alleyway, to pleasure the awaiting Deacon needlessly and without any delay.

That was ok, Deacon would do that if he let him. Preferring to be submissive. Too mild-mannered, too nice to be the one giving the orders.

And fuck he would listen if he did!

The man's pleasure would be his gain. Almost tasting it there in his mouth. Sucking it like a large, dripping ice lolly.

The guy still turned his blonde head to the side with a tilt and muttered something yet again. His attention thus left Deacon for a mere fleeting moment.

So, in those seconds, he found that he felt… surprisingly jealous. Jealous that the stranger was talking to another instead of him.

But who?

Still not seeing it. Not seeing anyone there.

Not liking the object of his affections being more into another though.

Because he had always been told that he was quite a catch, Deacon knew that body and look-wise he was, and he wasn't being vain by it. But Deacon always worried that he was – far too nice to be noticed by others.

And we all knew that good guys finished last.

Didn't they?

And where he wondered had the screaming woman gone that had led him to that eerie alley in the first place? Or was it the mysterious man that had pulled him there with his magnetic eyes? One who could even get a granny hot under the collar by his sure smirk.

Deacon didn't know. But by god, he would find out!

Even if it killed him, which it likely would.

Looking at the dashing dirty blonde as he nervously pushed his fingers through his thick, ruffled hair in a mere tizzy and hearing the rather gravely, sinful voice, it was surely not him who had screamed for help like a hassled, frazzled, scared woman had.

For he was all man.

Great.

That was what it was. Deacon had figured it out now that he had probed his mind for it.

Seeking an answer. The man of one's dreams whom he would naughtily have imagined would soon roughly take him by force there in the alley, bent him over the trash can like he were a rusty tin can, was – clearly on some kind of drugs, or mentally unwell.

Possibly both.

Deacon sighed in utter annoyance by this idea. Cursing his luck. He had never had any.

The guy was unaware or not showing it, just exactly the effect he was having on Deacon. Deacon feared that he could have carried a big, neon sign that said – fuck me! And he still wouldn't have realised.

Deacon knew this place here like the back of his hand having lived in the great city of Norwich his entire life, his home nearby there, so he knew that it was a dead end down there at the back of the alley. A massive wall with no way out to leave from.

Not that he wanted to. He wanted to stay there. Stay there with him. Forever.

No woman had come in to there – none had come out, so unless she had scaled the walls like Spiderman himself then...where the fucking hell had she gone to? Unless the stud before him had eaten her all up?

Deacon himself wouldn't have minded being eaten up by the guy either.

Heck, he would have offered himself up on a plate and handed over the knife and fork! And the sauce.

His cock wouldn't mind that one also. It pressed through his tight pants while he studied the guy's crotch area for a hint of a bulge hidden away there. He was sure he could see one, but it may be wishful thinking on his part...

What would the guys be like, he wondered? Bigger than his? Smaller? Thicker? As long as his arm were...

The guy was still muttering along to himself as if it was an everyday occurrence that he did so, whilst Deacon was frozen in shock still at what he had discovered on his journey home. Staring frantically at the other man for some signs of sanity in there.

One dashing male of similar height and weight to him, but slightly bigger as he liked it, but who seemed to have a hidden power somewhere inside himself.

Deacon couldn't see it. No.

But – he could feel it as if it was surrounding him in its grip, reaching in, and taking his soul out with invisible hands. He yearned for the other like nothing he had ever known before. He needed this man right here and it stumped him – why?

The guy had on a simple grey hoodie and fitted indigo jeans that hung loose on the hips, while he himself had his crimson one on and dark cargo trousers to match.

Deacon's ears pricked up as he then heard a flutter and a woman's voice speaking again nearby.

Right there. Right near!

He looked around but was still stumped as he still saw – no one.

Just the two.

Two lost souls, would they be united?

The guy in front seemed to be getting more and more frantic. Grabbing onto thin air again. Flapping his arms up and down like a trapped bird would.

Groaning in need. Groaning at Deacon apparently.

He couldn't actually want Deacon also… could he? Deacon tried not to get his hopes up.

He doubted it.

That would be like an amateur model dating a demi-god and to have Stevie and then this dude strongly interested in him in one evening.

No one was that lucky…

"Fuck, she got away!" The intriguing guy muttered to himself with a final frantic flap. "Oh, well now she is not needed here I suppose. I have bigger fish to fry."

Zoning in on Deacon now like a predator. A hot one.

Fish to fry? Why, did he work in a chippy or something?

"Well then this is my turn to leave," Deacon said as he eyed the stranger and then backed slowly away from him and his hardened, wild stare that saw right through him.

Rather like one of his crazed patients – Mr Huggy. Who was anything but even remotely huggable. Touchable. This was what this guy would be if he were a deranged dog in person form.

Handsome but surely – deadly.

Getting ready to take a run the heck out of there, Deacon, urged his body to pick up the message that he needed to leave there for home!

But… it still failed him.

He had gone down there to help someone in desperate need.

Now it was he who needed the help it seemed.

The stranger spoke again in his gruff, hot voice, "You can see me? I am not imagining this?" He asked Deacon curiously intensively.

Nervously. An accent similar to Deacon`s, but the voice far rougher than his.

He liked it. He truly did. It sounded like someone who smoked over fifty a day would sound. Throaty. Deacon was too healthy for all that.

"Yes…" Deacon replied unsurely. Now fidgeting as he stood.

Feeling like that was maybe the wrong answer for him to give him. He was clearly unwell, that he could see. He didn't want to set him off.

Make him pounce.

Mmmm. Tempting.

See him?

Of course, he could bloody see him! Why on Earth wouldn't he be able to see him? It was not like he was invisible…

The man strode nearer to him with long strides and long-toned limbs. Muscled arms swinging.

Now not so frantic behaving, now more surer and calmer. He groaned at Deacon as if he was feeling pleasure by just him being there in his presence – or maybe even pain.

Both ideas sounded good to him. As long as the man remained vocal.

Curious eyes flickered crimson again. With black.

The blonde shuddered as he finally reached the shuddering auburn one, "Well, then if you can see me then it looks like I will have to be back for you…" The man on reaching the startled vet nurse, then carefully reached over and brushed Deacon's hair out of his startled eyes and bit his lip, groaning loudly again as if he was in a cheap porno.

Deacon would subscribe to that.

He had seen plenty in his time and he guaranteed that this fascinating, but bizarre male would outshine them all.

Not clearly realising how hard that minor touch on his hair made Deacon, as his cock bulged fully erect in his boxer-like pants. Threatening to burst from his loose cargo trousers and ploughed there right into him. Not liking it either that he was attracted to such a weird, weird guy, who should have cringed him the fuck out by now and make him scarper from there.

To head home.

Give him the ick.

But didn't.

Because he was weird. And that made the auburn-haired one super uneasy, truth be told. Why couldn't life be normal for a change, he asked himself? Always something unexpected cropped up and shat on him from a great and utter height. Deacon himself strode slightly back and got into defensive mode while the guy remained like a striking tiger. Now not wanting to break eye contact with the other guy, fearing that he shouldn't.

He mustn't.

Although his body urged him to in every way.

It cried for him to.

He was now he decided to do something that would make him appear to be rather weak, but survival mode had now truly kicked in and the panic made sweat drench his skin even as he hummed with need and want for this man.

So, Deacon cried out, "Wh…what do you mean you will be back for me? I didn't see anything. I will forget everything that I witnessed here. I promise you!"

He gestured urgently with his bare hands that he would keep to his word even if it was the very last thing that he did.

Worrying that this mad, magnificent – no still mad man

would hurt him. He was a similar size and height, but he knew that he couldn't take him.

If they were sub and Dom there was no way that Deacon would be the Dom…the blonde reeked of it.

But the guy rushed out with now great speed and gripped one gesturing, shaking hand with his own one. Then sniffing it.

Clutching the startled Deacons hand as if he let go then so would he.

Gripping it harder. It was like his nails became claws.

What the!

Crimson eyes and now a lisp to his words as if something was filling the alley hanging out, guy's mouth.

The male spoke huskily- but surely, "You did see something. That means that you are. Mine. All mine. I could eat you up here and now, but I won`t. I will save that for later." Licking his lips.

A growl that if it wasn't so fierce and dominating to hear, that it would have made Deacon bust a nut or two right there in an explosion in the gloomy, smelly alley.

He would cum all over the bins that leaked ooze. Leave his mark there for the other to find him.

Forget that this guy was, frankly, fucking crackers! Now it appeared so, was he...

"I. Am. Not. Yours."

Deacon argued back. Not believing the rushed words that came out of his own mouth. And before he could reply, when he had started to think that maybe it was he who was the one that was unwell or had, had his sports water spiked by another for him to act this way entirely.

A shadow appeared behind him.

He knew that someone else was behind him - he could feel them. The question was, was it friend or foe? It couldn't get any worse right now.

Could it?

"Hey, there. You ok mate?" An inquisitive voice asked from behind with a twang to his accent.

A hint of Australian?

Deacon peered over his shoulder cautiously with narrowed eyes. Hoping that it was not someone behind him who could whisk the handsome man away from there, away from him, and leave him standing there all alone.

Or who in themselves could be a threat to either one of the two men who throbbed with a connection of sorts between them.

The stranger, the first one, as odd as he was – he knew they meant no harm to him.

He could see it by his slightly stubbled face. Feel it by his gentle touch. A touch he wanted more of.

Yearned for it.

Would this new man be a threat?

He sighed on the realisation that it was a local man that he briefly recognised from the local pub, who now tilted his head at him in silent question. Slim with salt and pepper hair of around the age of forty. He had a mature, stern face and green eyes that zoned right in on you.

Like they were now.

Deacon did know that he looked rather suss hanging around all the filth and rubbish apparently on his lonesome...

The pubgoer whispered, his think lipped mouth surrounded by stubble, "I thought I heard a woman screaming down here, but apparently there's not? Do you know anything about that?" Glancing suspiciously at Deacon and then eyes diverting towards the unknown as if it was him that was up to nonsense down there in the creepy alley.

And not another.

One could only hope... but if there was any nonsense that Deacon could get up to it would involve him and the dirty blonde with his trousers around his ankles and a good filthy hard seeing to for all the world to hear.

That wasn't going to happen!

And the pub goer long out of there… Deacon did not share his men, and he doubted with the fierce possessiveness aimed his way that the other guy, the cute, possibly psycho blonde did either…

He did not appear happy to see the new man near them. His face only softening when looking right at Deacon.

"It was him," Deacon whispered back with a small, polite nod. Not sure that dobbing in the blonde, delicious hottie who grew wide-eyed at this revealing statement and took a few startled strides back from him, was the best bet around. Eyes still trained on the nervous Deacon, who was regretting being so heroic now and vowed in the future he would mind his own business and let things be when he next heard things kicking off.

Confusion met the local, "Who? There is nobody there?" The Aussie seemed puzzled by this mere statement.

"He cannot see me, my little mortal."

Said the blonde in explanation in a hushed whisper that melted Deacon with his silky tone. "Only you can."

But before Deacon could speak, reply to either of the men, the angelic, possibly demon-like guy grew dark, delicious wings as black as the night before them - and flew away into the sky.

He fucking flew!

Flew off. With fucking wings... Deacon screamed in surprise at the gorgeous wings that left the handsome man's back in a smooth glide, while the Aussie remained completely un aware of this. Ones that lifted the slightly muscled blonde off of the bare ground and he left the alley like a graceful bird. And not one of his imagination.

But not before the husky male spoke clearly to him in a stifled warning, "Remember who you belong to. My sweet mortal mate. Any who try to take you from me will pay the price..."

As the two men left, stood there looking at each other stumped for words in total disbelief, the Norfolk one and the Aussie one together, even though only one had seen the blonde there before their very eyes, for only they could, then they had both certainly just heard him loud and clear. Crystal clear even.

For surely two could not imagine the same thing being said by another?

There was only one question on their mind.

What the actual hell?

CHAPTER TWO

<u>Now</u>

<u>Fess</u>

With all his narks and flaws the handsome, but certainly in now deep shit Vamp, stood up tall and proud and looked at the one who could end him right there and now, head-on through crimson, stormy and furious eyes.

Daring him to retaliate in any way.

Daring him to deny everything that he had apparently done to him.

The one who had all the power in this place and time. Not Fess, no, but another– him.

Rhys.

One of the oldest vampires in the whole Vampire realm high in the sky, a realm only entered by immortal beings and so Rhys was one of the most powerful vampires that existed in all of time.

Certainly, one of the craziest vampires out there.

This was his territory that surrounded them both. Fess was merely for that moment - a guest of the older males. A friend if you like.

It seemed not so any more with the unwaning actions that he had taken back when that had now deeply offended Rhys.

The dark soulless castle that now stood in all its glory bared down on the one who should be now truly frightened by his own mistakes.

When all he felt here was numb...

There had been a few errors that Fess had made and now they had firmly caught up with him... his past clutching him in its stony grip, not wanting to let go.

It showed him what he had not long had.

Now Fess - had nothing.

Nobody.

No.

Not even the gorgeous enticing human who he had at first thought was his ex-Elfina's second mate, the ex who he had kidnapped and wrestled to that human alley.

Iden was her first mate, but which would be preposterous as vampires usually only had the one!

Ok. They always had the one...no exceptions.

The annoying ex that he had just gone and bloody taken for reasons that he now could not explain, but who had hence gotten away from his claws, as Fess was far too busy gawping at that maddening, but sweet-smelling human in that Norfolk alley near where he had grown up, to keep hold of her!

That wonderous male that had gotten beneath his skin. Who smelled divine.

Fuck...he cursed again internally.

Feeling like he could die in agony at the distance between him and what he now knew to be his right – feeling the heartbreak before him.

His shameful secret – obsessed with a mere human.

A man.

Mated to one it had turned out to be when he had always assumed it would be to a woman.

One that had made his cock so fucking hard like a large, chiselled rock and his balls so tight until they clenched.

For how could he who used to be an out-and-out ladies' man when he was alive, he would admit to that, be fated mates with a mere human – male instead of a female?

He couldn't, he just couldn't.

Impossible! Unlikely even.

But it wasn't…the signs had been there, big, huge ones, he just hadn't seen them with his eyes wide open. Now they were.

Open wide and ready to see all of him.

He groaned again at the enticing man's scent that still laced his lightly-haired skin; it had clung to it like a second one would. There must be some mistake somewhere! He would never live it down if the others, the other vamps, his ex, and her stupid mate ever found out who he was now lusting over.

Not that he would be living for that much longer if Rhys had his way with him right about then. So, Fess knew that he had to leave the human the heck alone for his own safety, couldn't even try to get to know him in any way possible, as a friend- nothing more… nothing less.

Although he urged inside to claim him.

To leave his mark on that gorgeous neck of theirs.

He had to have nobody.

But Rhys.

His former boss, the king of the darkness, the one who wanted to make him suffer in every vile way that he possibly could – he wanted to make Fess scream with agony until pain left his lips, as the blaze blazed in and took him away from what he was used to the most.

Rhys would stand and watch and feel no remorse to it. The baddest of the bad.

The lowest of the low.

But, yet Fess had acted worse.

Far worse.

He had fucked up – big time, he could now hold his hands up high into the vampire realm's cloudy air and admit that he had done. He had done a bad thing, no lots of them - and here in the darkness where they both now stood eye to eye, there would be no forgiveness from his previous former friend.

Here, there would be no mercy for him.

From him.

Fess knew that he could either take what was coming to him and accept that it would happen now or – roll over and simply die - horribly. Which as an immortal vampire was only possible in one of two ways. Both were as gruesome and grizzly as they came. Both were something that no one, no vamp wished upon their worst enemy, not even on Rhys. Beheading was his first lovely option.

Fess had seen it done; he wanted no part in that. Although one would not realise that one's head had come clean off of their body until it rolled right there at their feet, their eyes glazed in fright – then it would be too late.

Much too late.

The last option to kill a vampire was – pure flickering fire. Flames that burned right down to the core and that licked at one's skin until they were simply no more. Fess himself knew that he had never killed a vampire, heck, he had never killed a human either.

Ok, he was lying to himself.

He had…but by Rhys stance – he might as well have killed all of his entire family and all his own clan, instead of Fess turning the older ones human mate into a vampire with the way that he was now frantically clenching his fists angrily Fess`s way and gritting his sharpened teeth, secretly preparing, plotting, to wipe him out for good with his magnificent dark magic.

Fess had upset his mate, Rhys`s Justina, and therefore in that act – he had upset him in every way possible that there were.

"Well, if I am going to go out, then I will go out with a bang," Fess smirked at the older one with a shrug.

Ignoring the shudder that threatened to creep in.

Trying to come to terms with the fact that this time when he actually died – there would be no resurrection.

This time he would be snuffed out from existence like a bad smell that encased it whole.

"That you will." Scoffed Rhys looking bored at his hands.

Rhys was always so dramatic!

His long dark hair flowed in the wind. Eyes narrowed until they were just merely just slits like a un nerved tiger. He had always held such power before he had added to it with dark magic that he had stolen from the realms.

Fess argued back with his former boss although he knew that it was meaningless to even try to, "How could it be known that the day I massacred a load of people, turned them, that one would regrettably turn out to be your fated mate? No one could ever guess that. But no one."

It was true.

Fess had killed Justina, a nurse at the hospital where she worked in and brought her back to life to act as Vampire eye candy for him. When he was a ladies man and new vamp in one. Which had not gone to plan.

Unaware that ten years later that that move would now come back to bite him square in the ass.

She and all the others that he had turned had either died or rejected him. Gone their own ways.

Ungrateful…he could have simply drained them of their blood and left their corpses there on the ground for the rats to feast on! He wish he had now.

Rhys shrugged uncaringly. His face shifted with unpent rage at the slight to his female.

Still fucking handsome.

Still fucking deadly, as anything. Fess wished that he held that power in his grasp. But luck like that didn't behold him…

Cheeks puffed out in anger as Rhys clicked his tongue, "What is done is done, boy. But you still need to be punished for it, for your sins, Fess. If I didn't then Justina would never let me touch her again. It is me or you and you are worthy of nothing, but pain itself."

Was he?

He was beginning to think so. Maybe he should just have died that day in the car back when.

"Punished. I can handle that." Fess said straight-faced with a bead of sweat dripping down him. Now thankful for the plead of Rhy`s Justina, and her stuck-upness but honestness that he may live to feed from a human another day.

Until the older, angrier vamp said with a hiss - "With death."
Rhys sprang out adding with a ghastly inhuman growl, one
that rivalled a rabid wolf.

Ok, maybe not… it seemed that no matter what he said to
Rhys, Rhys was not hearing his words aloud and taking any
notice of them. He may as well have been talking to himself
the whole darn time that he had staked his plea. Still, Fess
had no regret about what he had done back then as a newer
vamp.

A recently turned one.

For he couldn't. That was not who he was now not so much,
but it was who he was then. The human that he was mated to
should fear him. Bow down to him. Shown who was the
boss.

 But he, that glorious human male was the only one who he
would never hurt.

Killing a load of people in a decade for blood, for company.
Money.

For power. Pretty ones that couldn't fight back no matter
how much they wanted to try to. Or they wouldn't even
bother to try. Not expecting to win.

He had a type.

The weak did not grow to be strong. They slithered along without hope and died in a sea of flames. A bit like what was coming to him now.

For wasn't it true that Vampire`s did what they had to do to survive in any way that they could?

They had to. For it wasn't easy being the Walking Dead. The only thing that he now regretted was that he hadn't found out the human man's name before he perished. The gentle one in the manky alley who lit up the dingy place like it was Christmas.

Who smelled like a thousand roses.

Well, there could only be one man, one for him now. He regretted that he hadn`t taken those soft lips with his rougher ones, pressing that stubbled face with his own and laying claim to his frazzled human.

He and he alone.

Turned his whole being human upside down by his vampire one.

Them together to face the world as one. A bond like no other, but one of the fated that they were.

Fess could do a thousand wrong things in his lifetime, in his ten years as a vamp, but that was the only thing that he would ever regret to this day personally. Not knowing the auburn, dark-haired warrior's name.

He was so fucking beautiful.

Lucious eyes lined with long eyelashes that took in his every move when he had stood there in shock.

A lean figure, but Fess could tell that the human who had caught his attention had worked out at the muscles there on his arms as if he lifted weights. He could smell the deodorant that the enticing human wore, but also noticed the slight natural musk of sweat that lingered there after a likely hectic workout.

He could lick it up. Enjoy the taste on his lips. Human sweat. Human enjoyment.

He wished that daring man who thought he was saving a woman could be his workout…give those thick, though toned thighs some use.

And now it was too late…far too late. He hoped that the guy would forgive him when Fess`s death broke the bond that was there between them.

Move on and be happy with another.

No, fuck that, he raged!

He felt a twinge jut through his heart at the thought of it. If he still had a working one.

No. Anything, but that. No one could take their bond apart and make it their own.

Nothing could ever compare.

For how could it? They had a dark, delicious destiny between them.

"You would understand if you had your own mate." Rhys taunted to the waiting Fess. He seemed to be enjoying himself a bit too much. A voice full of ridicule. Glee with his taunting words.

But oh, Fess knew. He just wished he had done.

He was not going to answer that, tell Rhys that he had a mate of his own to try to live for and that he did truly understand the mate bond now. He understood everything, completely, that the older vamp felt.

That if someone had done to his mate, man or not, unsure as he was, as Fess had done to Justina then Fess wouldn't have been as patient as Rhys was.

He would have killed the person long ago if he could have laid his claws on them. He would have drained their blood dry and pissed on their grave.

Laugh while doing it.

Do it again for kicks.

But now he had to meet his doom.

It was what was owed to him. What he deserved in every way.

Fess was turned by his sire Iden, ten years back. Then after Iden having found out what he had done to those people whom he had classed as mere mortal innocents, those weak women, the turnings that had gone wrong, because turning a vampire was not as easy as one may think, and also Rhys having fallen out with his brother Iden of course – for good, Rhys and Fess had both been banished from the vampire realm.

For good.

With one last chance.

The earth was no home for them so there was only one place that they could go – the darkness itself. And it was exactly like it said on the tin.

A dark like no other.

The darkness. A small part of the vampire realm off limits to the rest of the vamps and their magnificent, honest, soul collecting. Those too pure of heart to be there in the dark. Set even one foot there, one toe.

It could make you mad, and pull you right in, but the two and a few others managed to find a way to stabilise themselves so that it did not affect them all too much.

Only a little.

Still carrying on their soul-collecting journeys to avoid annihilation because that was what they were created for. Knowing that any visitors that visited or attempted to break into Rhys`s gloomy castle at the edge of the realm, would either succumb to the madness – or from a dark power that was like no other.

Hidden security.

The other option except beheading, the only other way to kill a vamp was - fire. This was also an option that Fess really wanted to try to avoid as his old friend, well kind of… glared at him with nothing, but malice in his now shady blackened narrowed eyes. But one that with Rhys and all his dark magic practising that he was aware of knew there was a strong likelihood of it occurring.

He had seen the fireballs that Rhys liked to throw at those that were not quick enough or who he felt had pissed him off. Heck, he had had one or two thrown his way and managed to swerve them just in time. But this time Fess knew that a fireball would be the least of his worries as Rhys sized him up for a fitted death suit.

And that was when it happened before he even had time to think, to act, react, before he had time to plan his next move, to maybe beg the older man, vamp, for mercy.

Flames shot through the air from Rhys`s turned-out palms, the dark magic that no one spoke of it shot straight for him. Fess even with his vamp speed had no time to dodge, no time to escape, so instead he quickly got himself into a curled-up ball, defences up, and tried to protect himself in the best way that he could do – but failing so miserably.

Now his whole back was ablaze as the older vamp simply sneered in disgust at the sight of it and then walked casually off while Fess begrudgingly got ready to meet his end in a fury of orange light.

Being burned alive.

What a horrible way for one to go. Closing his eyes to and praying for a quick end to the pain that burned from the outside and then back into him. But now that he was dead he knew that there was no god – but a higher being that no vamp was aware of.

But that existed.

Rhys left Fess there all alone, burning, not caring as he left that the smaller vamp who had served him so well, who had been his friend when no one else would was burning in agony, not caring, or even seeing that Fess fell straight to the ground in a crippled heap.

Clawing to get up. Hungry to.

But then Fess felt a power surge like no other rip through his dying again, soul.

He had to get up, he had a mate now to think of, take care of, as the one that would take care of him right back there in return. Maybe not the one that he would have chosen to be his because that would surely have been a woman, wouldn't it?

But – destiny itself had done.

As he burned, began to slowly waste away into nothing, the flames licking his crumpled once stunning, magnificent body - needed to man up, and be strong because the thought of not getting one final glance at the gym-going curious human before he truly died ate him there alive.

The thought hurt him more than the fire did as he screamed and as he burned.

Fess frantically jumped up, trying to put the flames on his torso out, and unleashed his glorious wings to break free of it, be free. Get out of there.

Right back down to Earth…

Where he had first come from.

CHAPTER THREE

<u>Now</u>

<u>Deacon</u>

That night as the flap of wings disappeared with the handsome, dirty blonde-haired male, he had worryingly exchanged looks with the other guy that he briefly remembered who he had come to learn was called simply - Ru and then had left the smelly alley.

But not before asking Ru with curiosity, "Did you hear that man's voice just then, Ru?"

A good question. Had he?

Not wanting to have been the only one that had of done because that was a one-way ticket to madness.

And no one had time for that. He had animals to save, and people to please. Deacon was a people pleaser through and through.

Ru nodded.

He had! Thank god! Allies! He replied in his startling, Australian twang.

"I did. I heard a woman`s voice and then right after - a man`s. Couldn't see a dicky bird though. Freaked me the fuck out mate, if we are being honest here. I have heard rumours about things that could not be explained, unseen people, but I never believed them. Never wished to."

He was not the only one.

Deacon knew without even looking into a mirror that he was now pale as come be by the events of that night. So, pale that only a good tan could fix it.

Or a good fucking by one guy in general...one guy alone.

Oh god. He had it bad.

"Me too." Deacon didn't know what all this was, this eerie shit, as he shut his eyes and took a deep breath he knew it would haunt him forever. Remembering he wasn't alone he opened his eyes - feeling a fool, he muttered politely for Ru to take care of himself, he would catch up for a pint soon to discuss things, feeling that he had a new ally, so he wasn't alone with this, and then hot-footed it out of there as quickly as his body would let him.

No longer anchored to the ground now that the hot, winged, fantasy guy had left.

His mortal? What did that even mean?

"That was some freaky shit mate," Ru frowned. He looked spooked. He didn't blame him for he most certainly did! Deacon had also heard rumours himself.

A vet – Vik, whom he occasionally worked with and who had some far-out ideas going on had told him the rumours about invisible folks. Unseen people.

Apparently, according to Vik, some people had been attacked, taken by invisible forces unknown and who were unseen to them.

Some had been bitten and left on the streets to be found by others with bites to the necks. One local man had snuck into his exes flat and whilst alone he had suddenly taken a nose dive out of a first-floor window.

He has been pushed – clear as day.

CCTV didn't lie.

Brains splattered onto the pavement so all could see his weak mind and stalker ways.

Some according to his colleague Vik, were never to be seen again. Vanishing into the night - grabbed on a night out. Deacon had dismissed the whole crazy idea of it as Vik was into whacky ideas and conspiracies, so he wasn't the most reliable of gossips to begin to listen to. It was a bit like the boy that cried wolf.

As soon as Vi had started to go on about the earth not being round at all then this as when anything that he said here after was sadly ignored.

He was a good vet if nothing else though. But stark raving mad! Or was he…? Maybe he had something…

He eventually, shakily, got back to his run-down ground-floor flat and shut the door to with a loud sigh. Feeling for the first time – scared. Scared that he lived there alone and also scared as the other apartment remained empty.

Then with thoughts racing, he walked to the bathroom and ran himself a hot shower. Wanting to clean himself up from the dirty way that he felt and not just from the rubbish.

He gently took his soft-smelling clothes off and he shivered as the temperature dropped.

Then got into the shower in a hurry as his skin cooled down. Enjoying feeling the warm, running water that ran over his skin now instead of the cold air. Soothing it.

 But there in the warmth of the shower was only one guy that was there on his wondering mind.

He doubted there ever could be another. It was as if they were forever linked, forever more.

Stevie J, now firmly thrown out of his thoughts for the wolves to feast on.

Him. That blonde, divine being.

He did not even know his name for him to speak aloud with orgasmic words, and to roll his glorious name over his thick tongue. Only that he could not be seen by another- only him, and that he had – wings and a hidden power that encased him from the tips of his gorgeous thick hair to the tips of his toes.

Deacon was not sure he could even now remember what footwear that the guy had had on as his mind had been busy elsewhere, but that. Not one to be obsessed with clothes in a way so that he would notice everything that someone wore. For he didn't.

He personally would rather have seen the guy naked and without a shred of clothes on as he beckoned him over with a tempting tease. He drooled now enjoying the distraction that the guy had brought him for a while.

The distraction from everyday boring life.

Had he imagined it?

No, no, how much though his thoughts to and fro he could not shake off the fact that the man had been so unworldly. Not appearing quite human at all.

Too perfect to be.

The wings were a hundred per cent real having just shot out of his back at the speed of light.

Then he flew away into the dead of night.

Deacon in his work, at the gym, had met a lot of people in his years. This guy outshone them all and that was not normal he did find. He had something extra about him. Wings. He was something extra!

As Deacon carefully soaped down his body a quick shower turned into a self-exploration expedition. His fingers lightly brushed past his now springing-out hard cock, which was now fully erect at the thought of the light-haired stranger from before.

Again. Who needed Viagra when you had a guy like that on your mind!?

 He started to rub some soapy lotion onto it as it sprung to life, starting off with light, tender strokes and then taking it harder, harder, harder! More.

Harder. He panted softly. Murmuring. Enjoying the feel of his own hand. Imagining another were there.

He groaned loudly and the noise echoed around the white walls of the bathroom. Thanking the lord that he lived alone because otherwise, things could be... awkward.

Imagining the guy gently touching his firm cock roughly with his own larger hand and then increasing the pressure until it tingled with need. He was wanting to erupt so darn badly until his cum splattered the shower walls, but he wouldn't.

Not quite yet.

The thought of the inhuman one rubbing his hard balls with his other hand and then also jacking Deacon off at the same time, until he eventually came all over him right there in the shower with no apology for it.

He was not the sort.

Deacon's cum would drip down the bad boy's face and he would then likely flick out a tongue to catch it in his awaiting mouth.

He would almost certainly drown in it, there would be that much. All for him. Only for him. Savouring the taste that was caused by only him.

Because that was all he could be, a bad boy! No innocent looked like that. Acted like that. A bad boy with wings that took him in the dead of the night.

With one more thrust into his own impatient hand, Deacon came hard for real, whilst wondering as the fireworks faded, would he see that man again?

Should he even want to…?

He left the shower whilst not even bothering to clean up, forgetting to or not wanting to and got ready for bed.

Knowing that it would be a night of no sleep for him.

There could be no other way…

The next day as the sun shone through the window he swung his legs out of the bed after an unsettled night as was expected by him.

He had had the craziest dream just then, one that made him feel sick to his stomach. Nausea washed over him as he sat up and it had unsettled him. He did not like the horrible sicky feeling that he had, had.

His dreams were usually pleasant ones. Sexual ones. This one – wasn't. It was anything, but that.

In the dream it felt like he was on fire, he could smell the char of his skin burning in pain and no one helping him as he screamed in agony.

Just a crumpled ball of fire. The fire became him. He was the fire.

He thankfully had managed to put the fire out, but after the flames had died then only his face, shoulders, and some of his arms and hands remained free from the totally searing, painful burns. The dream was so realistic that it was almost like – he had really been there.

He had even gone and checked in the mirror to make sure that it wasn't true! Crazy, he knew that. But that would be so fucking awful if it were that he couldn't possibly imagine. The strength of someone that did.

He heard a clatter at the window, then sighed. The bad side of living in a ground floor flat in a bad part of the city even though this specific window was at the back and was not faced.

He could not afford to get out of there and move somewhere better just yet all though he had plans to.

Walking over to the largest window in just a pair of shorts that hugged the curve of his ass, he looked out, but could see anything that should not be there. Nothing was out of place. His mind roared.

Shivering as a cool breeze hit him from out of the blue. It was like someone was watching him up close, but for now, they would remain faceless to him, and he would let them. If they existed, to begin with.

"I think I am going mad." He muttered to himself and wrung his hands, for there was no one else surely there. The other flat was uninhabited unless it had suddenly been let. Suspecting now that he was imagining things, hoping things, his mind was heated from that special encounter that had made his mortal heart pound.

So, then he surprised even himself when he quickly in just his shorts hopped back into his unmade bed and he then to his excitement – sprung his cock free from his awaiting tight pants that held it all in.

He sighed naughtily and bit his lip.

Then he worked his glistening cock once again with his awaiting hand. It was as if he hadn't touched it in days with how truly aroused that he felt.

 It throbbed with need. He could feel the heat brewing in his average-sized cock, but he wanted so much more besides. He wanted it to be elsewhere… wanted to have his ass filled and then fill their one back in return.

The man from the night before flew through his mind. He could almost taste him. Had he even been interested in Deacon, he wondered? But he could remember the burning desire in those yellow and then red-tinted eyes.

He carried on stroking the relief out of him. Fuck!

To his embarrassment, although there was no one there to see it, was there? He came rather too quickly for him. The quickest that he had ever come even when he was a mere teen.

Cum shot out from the head of his throbbing, glistening cock in a furious fountain.

He wanted to say the guy's name right there on his lips as he came, but then to his saddened dismay found that he couldn't say it. So instead, as he did Deacon simply yelled – "Fuck me, winged angel. The one meant for."

Feeling shame wash through him at saying that about a divine being – he was certainly going to hell for that.

But cuming over his angel, the one who had mesmerised him, nonetheless.

For what else could he be, but that?

An angel…

CHAPTER FOUR

<u>Fess</u>

With a startling crash, the badly injured Vamp fell to the earth as if he simply weighed nothing, but mere air. Cascading as he fell in a spiral through the darkening clouds. Past the birds. Planes and more besides it.

He sensed that his marvellous wings had only just made it down there with him as he landed on the earth and had only just carried his weight with them. And so, he was now thankful forever more that he had made it safe and sound there on the ground.

Breathing – if he could, a sigh of relief.

Supposedly this were much better that than being stuck in the vampire realm, being set on fire and before that - ridiculed.

Taunted. Tortured.

Up there he had felt so, so useless. Down on earth, he felt much more powerful. Stronger like he could take anything and fuck the world! Be anything that he chose to be.

Because he was.

He was. An invisible vampire after all could have deadly effects on the unsuspecting humankind if they made their power move when it was least suspected.

He did not know and was not too sure if he would ever fly again because he was so gravely injured as he studied his black wings with a lone hand. Trailing his fingers down them to see. There was no one there that could possibly be able to help him, to fix him, to fix them – no, not really – here he found sadly he was all alone with his problems.

It sucked.

Here he just had himself to guide him.

To plan his next move. To make one if he could.

Maybe Rhys had done him a favour? That older vamp, one of the oldest, was the only one to make him feel weak, although, given the older vamp's overpowering strength, it was with certainty that nearly all other vamps would shake in their wings once facing off to the oh-so torturous one.

Who wanted to kill them…

He knew no one down there on the chaos of the earth. Those he had, had all thought that he had died in the car crash that had brought him to knowing of the whole vampire world in the first place.

The only few people that he had were in the vampire realm which was high in the sky out of the human's interfering gaze, and a place that he was not sure that he ever wanted to go back to again.

No, not now. Too much had happened.

It had been a great and wonderful place where vamps could live and do their business in relative peace together.

Un disturbed.

Down on the ground, he was not seen by any mortal. He never had been, and he hated it with a powerful vengeance. They could feel him, smell him, sometimes if he chose to – they could hear him, but see him they could not.

Not as long as they lived or he.

And that to Fess who wanted to be seen by others, adored it, and wanted to be known was pure and utter torture. Even when he was alive he had had to push himself for anyone to take any notice of him, to do reckless things to ensure that he was right there in the spotlight where he felt like he belonged in.

But... that was what had gotten him into this whole, entire mess that he now found himself in.

Invisible to all as now a badly burned-out vampire. An eternal. The only one who would see him could see him, but wouldn't want to when they now saw the state that he was in now.

Chargrilled like a steak at a Barbie.

It didn't take a mirror to see what he would look like as he studied the scars right there on his upper arms that itched and tugged and wept.

Knew that they would run down his back like a snake slithering through the sand at the beach.

He could feel them. It hurt so fucking much. A weaker mortal would not have survived that pain, that excruciating pain. Couldn't have. would have wished not to.

He could feel it deep inside to his inner core. He glanced again at his arms, studying them carefully as the tears fell like a river, at the burns that raged openly down them that would never heal no matter how much of his depleting power he shot through them.

Forced it in to them. And he had tried.

No vampire magic or healing could rid him of the marks, the scars, the welts that would mark him for the rest of his days.

76

Mark him for what he was – simply nothing.

He whilst he was scanning the front of his body from head to toe turned his handsome head, at least something was still handsome he noted, as the struggling Fess felt someone's presence right near his very pained soul.

His stomach churned as their scent wafted in, in the breeze. The scent of alcohol hit his nose with a bump before anything else did so. If it was a human near him then there was no chance in the humans hell that he would be not able to help himself taking a spot of dinner right then.

So hungry that it hurt almost as much as his open wounds did from the beating, the punches, and kicks, that his nasty former boss if you like had inflicted on him in his rage. And the blood for sure could help with the pain that coursed through his body like a fiery dragon through the day-lit sky. But any raised hopes were dashed as soon as the shadow started talking.

And he smelt the sourness that only the un-dead could have. Barren. A fellow vampire soul collector.

He was so fucking angry it seemed which was unlike him, that Fess flinched once again. Barren said that he thought that Fess knew where his fated mate was – but honestly, he didn't. He didn't think so anyway. For he did not know who she was.

Had no intention to. Frankly, he did not care.

Rhys had behind his mate's back, behind every bodies back, set up a human blood farm down on earth.

With live hosts. They were kidnapping humans off the streets like nobody's business. More and more as of late.

The humans that were taken remained imprisoned to Fess's knowledge; their rich delicious blood was taken whilst they could not see their captors at all, only feel them.

Hear them.

Fear them...

Fess felt uneasy with the whole thing when he had first heard Rhys scheme for easy blood right there on tap. Without having to take it from the recently departed souls that involved them having to wait for someone to die.

Watching with trepidation as his boss's fridge was full to the brim with blood that shouldn't have been there in the first place. Too much for one vamp to consume. Coming from immoral means.

Not so much as he felt it was extremely wrong, but that he was also not sure what the punishment by those above them would be if those who were responsible got caught.

For when a vampire accepted immortality then they agreed to take the souls of the dead to meet their judgment. If they refused – they would be annihilated. He was lucky that he was banished before when he had fucked up that time and not just killed off.

He knew that there would be no second chances now.

He was just lucky that he was still alive.

And what would become of him now that he couldn't fly? Or he guessed that he couldn't. No way was he testing his precious wings out in front of a drunk, swaggering Barren who must have had a shit ton of booze for it to hit him even at all!

For vampires normally remained sober no matter how much they drank.

Barren angrily paced over to the other male his eyes alight. Knuckles clenching in sheer anger. Cracking them together. Obviously wanting to put the blonde one out of his fucking misery with his fists over and over again, until his vampire teeth fell out.

Although they would grow back. There was that.

Instead, the raging Barren touched Fess`s badly burned body – and shook him hard. Not caring that he was injured. But so bloody angry with him.

"Where did you get the blood in your fridge?" Barren yelled in anger as they came face to face. His posh voice quaking. Fess had never seen the mild-mannered one so enraged. He always seemed to get the blame for everything.

That didn't surprise him. This didn't surprise him.

Why couldn't he ask Rhys? Rhys would know. But it was clear as day – Barren was too scared of him. To him, Fess was weaker. And at the moment a push over.

"The blood?" Fess frowned collapsing onto the floor, his brows arching. Yes, he was currently weak.

"The blood in your fucking fridge at the castle! It was her! My mate! I drank my own fucking mate!" Barren on the search for his close friend Ruby, whom Rhys had taken, had stopped for a spot of stolen blood from Rhys`s castle.

Then realised that it was highly likely that the blood was off his soul's heart.

"Impossible." Fess spluttered. Wishing that he could sup his own mates blood. Amongst other things. The thought pleased him. It made this all worth worthwhile.

"That it is not. I know what I tasted. I know what I drank…" Barren gritted his teeth. If he continued he would need a dentist!

Fess shook his head.

"If you help me, I can help you find her." He offered. Not really believing his own words.

"So, you do know where the people blood farm is?" Barren probed with urgency.

"No…" Fess lied.

He had an inkling where it was. There were not many places that it could be. And he knew Rhys well.

"Like fuck I will help you then!" Barren scoffed, his eyes bulging. "Rhys was right. You are nothing! Just nothing!" He spat at Fess who wiped it away.

"Barren I am burned. Please. I need help." He pleaded with no shame.

Barren just looked at him like he was a piece of dripping shit on his shoe and flew quickly away from there leaving Fess alone and in agony.

He lay there for hours mumbling to himself and eventually fell asleep. Only to be awoken by – he sniffed – human blood. Walking and talking in - a live host. Now he was buzzing. This person, sorry mate! Was the answer to his problems. If he got enough blood then it would likely be enough to take him where he wanted to go.

Where he needed to go.

He had never gotten up so quickly in his entire life, he jumped up with all of his broken might. He scanned the place quickly. If he had a heart it would be racing right then.

A short distance away a man was walking down the road on his mobile phone. Face glued to the screen.

Before he could scream, before he could cry out, Fess had grabbed the startled phone addicted human, then progressed to nearly drain him of his blood, and so left the man there to die.

"Oops." Said Fess as he glanced at the stranger with no feeling. "Sorry again, mate." He licked the delicious blood from his lips not wanting to waste a drop as it tasted so darn good. He was going to leave the man alone, but then had a moment of clarity – deciding to tear the phone from the unconscious man's hand.

A pulse still beating - he could hear it. He did not want to get too close in case he was tempted to rip through his tempting main vein again before help could arrive.

See Fess wasn't that bad?

Not much…

"Your partner is hurt. They are at Rose Lane near the travel lodge. Hurry!" He growled into the phone quickly and then stomped on it so that he gathered he would not be traced.

Not that they could bloody see him anyway! He almost chuckled at that thought. What must the poor man think! Cursing his human for making him go soft and weak at the knees, the opposite of what he was usually like because before he wouldn't have done that with the blood-drained human stranger.

No way!

Now that Barren had gone who knows where, he tried his fragile wings to see if they could work again, hoping so desperately that they would do so, begging them almost, that they would take him from there – nothing.

They fluttered, there was slight movement, but would not move enough. He did not move an inch. His feet still firmly on the ground.

Great. It was just like being bloody mortal again...and that had sucked.

This was no better.

"Fucking wings!" He cursed as his marvellous wings took him to nowhere town.

He felt to his joy a little better now that the blood thrummed through him and gave him some much-needed energy. He sniffed, certain that he could scent the human man that belonged to him and only him, his human mate, who was taking over his mind, body and soul and making him ignore the scars there that lingered there like a tattoo on his skin. It was the only thing to stop him from thinking of them.

He started walking slowly and carried on with an ache in his gut. An hour later, probably less, as he reached the main part of the city, stopping every now and again his power fading, he reached a run-down block of flats that stood out like a sore thumb.

His nose instantly turned up in displeasure at the sight of the rundown buildings before him.

Vile! He had not grown up with money although he had near the end of his life, but this building was lower than he would ever dare to go!

"Now, my little fated mate. My little human. This will not do," Fess muttered as he took in where his fated lived with a dramatic shudder. He went off quickly towards the back of the horrid building and tried to look for a way inside it, but found that he did not have much luck at getting in.

He needed to get in!

Hmm. It appeared that it was locked to as he grasped the door handle with his quaking hand. Trying to be gentle so as not to arouse suspicion by his mate, or the neighbours.

Wanting to kick it in with all of his might, take what was owed to him.

Take who was made for him.

Take him hard right there at the door until he quaked beneath him like he was made to.

Damn it!

Looking upwards with a sniff it appeared that only the bottom flat was currently now in use. The top one seemed to be remarkably empty.

He didn't blame them. Who the fuck wanted to live there? Well empty except for maybe rats that was… his vampire hearing was right there at the top of them.

Senses excelled. He could almost picture their ratty scuttling from over there where he stood.

He could smell his future one like a perfect specimen though the dinge and the grimness of the building, he was there. So, fucking close to him, but yet still too fucking far.

He felt something strange run through him as he neared him. Excitement.

No, it could not be that!

Could it? It was there, there was nothing else that it could be, but he had never felt that emotion for, for a human or vamp. Only for a fast car, he had felt that feeling before.

The rush.

He loved cars and had hated that they were not there in the vampire realm.

They did not need for them there with their wings and overwhelming powers...

As the sky darkened and the night drew in, he soon passed out in a stolen tracksuit, with his broken wings wrapped tightly around him for some comfort.

Seen by none.

He was dead after all.

Waking up the next morning he groaned in realisation as he realised that it hadn't all been a bad dream, laying on the floor with a sharp crook in his neck. Instead, it was... a living nightmare and not a dream at all.

Great.

Glancing at his charred skin again and knowing that he was lucky to be alive after the burns that were inflicted on him...alive -Ish.

"You had better be worth it!" He muttered about his mate as he got slowly to his feet.

He was. He was sure of it.

Destiny was rarely wrong.

Nearly all the vampire/human mates that he had seen were so sickeningly besotted with each other that it made him want to throw up in his mouth.

If he could, but that was another thing that vampires didn't do.

Vomit. And here he was being besotted with his own one.

The one that Rhys could never, ever find out about...

Retracting his wings into his now scarred back, he tiptoed quietly over to the window without delay. There was a slight gap in the curtain he noticed with a sneering smile as he could now see right in if he squinted.

He leaned gradually forward and thus bumped his head on the window with a prang.

"Fuck!"

Fess cursed on impact as the glass came for his head. "Stupid ass, mother fucking window!" He cursed as he yelled, now hearing movement, and so ducked out of the way from near sight.

Crap.

So tempted to show himself right then to the human inside.

The one that he so desperately wanted.

God, he could feel him even through the thin glass that separated them from each other! He could shatter it! But that would shatter him. Could hurt him.

The dark-auburn-haired one went away from view and the movement slowed down. What was he doing? He looked to be getting ready for work?

 Where was that? Who did he work with?

Fess growled at the thought of the male, his male, with others, but him.

Possessiveness coursed through him.

Not in his lifetime! Fess might be coming down to the fact that he was now destined to a man for all of eternity and attracted so desperately to him that it cursed his soul more than being turned into a vampire had done.

But then whilst he observed the male putting his work things down onto the unmade bed, clad in just a pair of baggy shorts. Far too baggy for Fess`s liking. He wanted ones that moulded to his mate's ass like they were a second skin. So that he could spank him and feel every curve with his hand. Hard.

That had never been his thing. It was now. His dirty, dirty mate who brought out the beast in him.

Fess drooled with need as he watched his human with blatant desire.

Silently. Deadly. Like a predator.

Ok… he was definitely into the human. There was no mistaking it. He wanted the man, his ass… his cock… Everything.

His body did. His head was still not sure what it wanted or should so want. It was still so much to take in and in so little time that he felt over whelmed. He had never thought about a man like that, in that way. Had it been hidden in him all along, waiting to come out?

The guy as he watched silently, got back into his bed. Why was he getting back into bed he asked himself? Great, he had a lazy mate he would pay heed to that… but still, he was so tempted to join him in that messed up bed.

But then…

Oh, dear lord! It appeared to be to his shock a free peep show! Fess had been aroused many, many times, in his lifetime. With woman, and now with this man here who would be the last one that he desired as long as he so lived. He had never been so aroused as to see his mate playing with himself right there in front of him.

Fuck! Gorgeous. Simply gorgeous.

Unaware that Fess was watching him through the gap in the window. Getting off on him.

Hard as anything. He cock so hard it could break the window!

Now playing with his own one in return...

"Fuck!" Fess cried in a whisper. Gripping his thick, long cock with his right hand and gripping the wall with his left for balance. Claws leaving their mark.

As the man in the apartment came hard, unaware, so did he right there on the creamy house wall. Then slumping against the window defeated after.

His orgasm had nearly killed him off.

If he wasn't already dead that was...

As he waited for his dick to go down which wasn't complying - he then heard it -

"What the fucking heck!" The door to the flat opened with a fierce slam that shook the run-down converted house. Surprising that it didn't fall down.

Shit, shit, shit! Fess cursed internally, putting his cock away. Instantly soft. But now rising again as the human cursed under his sweet breath.

Down boy, down! Who needed Viagra when he had such a sweet-smelling male?

The guy turned and clocked him in an instant - eyes wild.

"You!" The tall, dark, and handsome one now wearing a bright purple t-shirt along with his cum stained shorts, shouted at him. Pointing a finger his way in agitation. Fess could smell the cum dripping down the firm thighs from there.

He clearly hadn't wiped.

The perks of being a vampire! Exceptional smell.

He wondered what it would taste like as his mouth drooled. He hoped that soon he would get the chance to find out exactly what it tasted like…

The other male was clearly pissed that he had been spied on, "Did you…did you see that? How did you know where I lived?" He gasped in wonder.

His lips in the shape of a o pouted. Hands-on his slight curved hips in dismay.

"Maybe a little…" Fess grinned mischievously. Clearly being honest. Eyeing the other man from head to toe. His cock perked right up again in a jiffy as he took in the enticing fragrance that wafted out of them. Almost forgetting his scars, the ones that would never fade no matter how much he tried to make them until the guy zoned in on them…

Eyes bulging in surprise at them.

At him. Fess did not like surprises or being at the mercy of them.

The one thing that he didn't want to get noticed was being looked at as if the guy had super x-ray vision. Fess had gone from a blatant 10 to in his opinion now a 3 with his scars…but luckily his face was unaffected by the fire.

His sweet, angelic face framed with dirty blonde hair that had before gotten him places.

As it would now.

That would have finished him off if that had been touched! Small mercies…

"Omg! What happened to you?" A mixture of emotions flitted over the other man who stood in his flat doorway now watching Fess. Leaning to on the wall where Fess himself had not long been leaning with said cock in hand.

Worry flickered, then something else crossed his cute ass features. Was that a look of repulsion that Fess saw there in his features?! It had better not be…he struggled with the whole, unnerving idea of that.

He guessed he owed some kind of explanation as to why he was there without going into the full grizzly details. Standing in front of the wet patch on the wall.

"I got burned. Set on fire. What else does it look like?" Fess snapped. Covering his body up more so the scars were mostly hidden from the other's view. The ones that tingled when touched.

Tingled near him.

The guy flinched visibly. Face blanching. His small nose scrunched up.

"Well, I…"

"Save it! I don't need your pity. We can't all be as perfect as you! Can we?" Fess hollered in outrage, shaking his fist to make a point. He would never use it on him, just the wall. Though he would not be pitied by anyone.

Especially not by his deliciously handsome mate. The one who should accept him, warts, flaws, and all. Because everybody had them. And did he not realise who was in charge here between them? Who would always be in charge until their days there were ended?

Him. Fess.

No one else. Fess.

Him. Fess grimaced again. Feeling offended, feeling like oh, he didn't know! Pissed off right about now.

The guy said something unexpected.

"You… you… think I am perfect?" The dark-haired one blushed a vivid shade of red. An excited glow washed over his lightly tanned cheeks.

Either from a bottle or the hint of the sun. Fess went from complete and utter fucking outrage at being pitied to feeling something that he had never felt before in his whole, entire life.

Something undeniable.

All gooey inside.

Practically melting on the inside at his sweet ass humanly, refreshing adorableness. He did not like this one bit, this soppy lark!

Darn it! What had he done to him? It was he who should hold the power here and not the human with the sweet sincere blush.

"Yes." Fess said in explanation. "I was accused of something bad by another, set on fire and then sadly left for dead. Yada yada. I escaped there and returned here. I have nowhere else I can go to. I nicked this outfit as mine was fucked. So…"

Gesturing at said t-shirt and shorts black tracksuit.

"Omg! Shouldn't you be in a burns unit or something?" The human gasped.

Fess started laughing hysterically like a madman at this notion. The idea of it cracked him right up. He laughed again for dramatic effects.

Wickedly. Yes, he could do that, rock up at a human burns unit by his tod. But he would remain invisible to them so it would be as pointless as a pointless pencil to even set foot in there.

Also, he would be tempted to eat them all up. He now doubted the bemused human got the joke even if he did.

"What's so funny?" The human narrowed his eyes in all seriousness.

"It is an inside joke. Don't worry yourself, little human." Fess grinned trying to lighten the mood between them.

"Human..." The guy paled.

"Very."

"Are you not cold?" A flicker of sweet worry. "It is cold right now."

"We don't, I mean I don't feel the cold..." Fess explained.

"Oh." There was that cute nose wrinkle again.

"I don't feel a lot of things." Because he didn't.

"Oh."

Now cursing that he said that. He sounded like a nutter! He was a cold stone-dead vamp. But he didn't want to appear as one. If the guy closed in he would not hear the throb, throb of his heart beating. There was no air leaving his mouth, or his nose. There was a darkness in his eyes.

But Fess still could love if given the chance.

Hoping so. Wanting so.

It was time to take a chance, "Aren't you going to invite me in to your home then lad?" Fess asked moving forward to stake his claim to the superb male at his near touch.

Shoulder to shoulder. Flesh to flesh.

Wanting to take a nibble of this sweet delicacy. Lick up every drop and not dare waste any.

Introductions were in order as he openly stared, "It is Fess, by the way. What is your name, handsome boy? I have been wondering that since we last spoke..." Curious eyes locked onto his.

"Fess..." Said with more of a zed sound than a sss one.

"Yes."

"Deacon. Though I really should not be giving a random stranger my name. Especially one who wanks right at my back window and watches me doing so also." Deacon now scarlet looked from left to right as if to make sure that they were not currently being overheard by another. Letting out an embarrassed gasp at being caught in the act.

Fess pretended to cough, stifling a chuckle beneath it.

The answer – to deny everything!

"Wanks at your window! Outrageous! As if I would do something as awful as that!" Fess scoffed. "Though I would prefer the back door to the window, that from what I can see seems a far spectacular view…" Flickering eyes from north to south.

Brazen was an understatement.

"So, you didn't?" Deacon crossly shot out and eyed the vamp, unaware still that he was one. But as sharp as his words were, Fess could see the struggling human's words and face softening into something else.

"Urm… can I come in?" For once the vamp was lost for words, had not been interested in anyone since Elfina over ten years back. Even then it was not like this.

This intensity.

 This want and need. The madness that thrummed deep within.

She had been something pretty to have there by his side. Good company also although she had not savoured the limelight in the same way that he had.

This mortal was far more.

Pretty, cute, easy going it seemed. With a blush that made a warmth appear in Fess`s very core. One long forgotten about. His little blushing human.

Forever more.

The human was fighting a losing battle with himself, which was clear for all to see if there was anyone around that were. "Fine." Deacon replied with a sharp scowl and then moved to get out of the way of the chipped door frame so that Fess could then squeeze by him.

But the eager visitor still did not pass him by as a good guest would.

Fess was not good though. Never had been - and never would be.

Deacon could clearly feel slanted eyes burning into his back. "I have work in less than two hours though, so this had better be quick."

For it must. Deacon liked to be punctual.

Pah!

"I don't do quick." Fess flirted back cattily.

Deacon's eyes nearly bulged out of his head at this, and he quickly shut the door to behind them so that they were not disturbed. Not knowing whether he was letting a wolf through his door and he was liable to get bit.

If his mother actually gave a shit she would have done what all mothers had done and likely warned him not to talk to strangers. To certainly not let any in.

And here he was about to invite one into his home.

When he was alone. The thought that they had mutually masturbated turned him on when it should disgust him…

Sex at the forefront of his mind like a naughty teen reading a readers wife magazine that they had found under their dads mattress.

But then as the door closed to – Deacon was pushed, yes pushed into his own home as he was grabbed hard and thrown around as if by a bandit making haste from there.

And he found to his shame that he liked it.

Really fucking liked it.

Deacon was more aroused than ever before, and this weird man – yep still weird, cute, just did something to him that no one else had done before.

Could ever do before.

Like they were tied together with invisible threads that forever linked them as one.

Entwining them. Combining them. Like they had known each other forever and ever, but they possibly couldn't have although it seemed like it. A unique feeling that words could never describe.

Only feel.

At the handsy invasion, "Hey, what the!" Deacon`s words stuck in his throat as Fess went and kissed him so extremely hard, grabbing his face in possession as if he wanted to draw the breath from his very lungs. So, fucking hard that it was like he was the one that was burned instead of he.

Tongues entwining in tandem. Their movements in sync.

"Oh!" Deacon murmured happily.

Hornily.

Not expecting this at all on a day like this, but instead going along with it anyway. He groaned as the kiss continued on with sheer urgency and Fess started pawing at him with desire like nothing else before.

He could feel his cock rising. Heck they both were. Rising together!

Ripping at his t-shirt. Taking it off. Ripping at his shorts. Until they came apart at the seams. It seemed he had a strong one there!

No one would have guessed that Fess had not done this before with another male by his every confident action. Even he was surprised at the overwhelming urges that shattered his soul by being within an inch of this heaven itself, urges that made him not give a fuck about what he was currently doing right now with someone of the same gender as he were.

For now, was the time to be bold, "Come." Said Fess taking Deacon`s smaller hand with his own and leading him straight towards the awaiting unmade bed.

Teasing Deacon. Turning him around. Kissing his neck roughly. Scenting his neck. The one that throbbed with his favourite vein.

Deacon's heart raced again as Fess's lips trailed along his neck, leaving a trail of fiery kisses in their wake. He groaned. The room seemed to spin around them both, the only constants being the heat that consumed them and the sound of their ragged breaths in the enclosed room.

Fess's hands roamed over Deacon's body with an urgency that matched the intensity of their kiss.

As they tumbled onto the bed in a flurry of pawing still, Deacon felt a mix of excitement and apprehension flood through him. He had never experienced anything like this before with anyone, this raw lingering desire that surged between them and he doubted that Fess had done either.

His mind was now reeling, trying to process the overwhelming sensations that coursed through his veins. From just someone that he had encountered down a dark alley to being seconds away naked in his bed.

The bed that had not had another man in it in a long time, if ever...

In a frenzy, Fess peeled off his own clothes kicking them away, the ones that hid his flaws, whilst maintaining eye contact with Deacon at all times, not wanting to lose it not for a nanosecond, as if silently urging him to do the same as he. Their gazes locked together in a potent blend of desire and uncertainty.

Deacon hesitated for a moment, clearly thinking things through. His mind was surely clouded with doubts about how far he was willing to go with this odd, but simply overwhelming man. Not quite aware that they were soul mates. Although likely feeling it with every bone in his fragile, human body.

But when all thoughts rapidly flew out the window as a needy Fess started to finger his ass gently.

He gasped.

Adding more and more fingers each time until the searching vamp could not possibly fit any more in to the pert humans bum.

"Your ass is so tight for me," Fess whispered.

Such a filthy, filthy mouth.

He knew that he wanted this strange, strange man, the one with the blatant wings. Why did he have wings again?

Heck – he had forgotten about that. But, damn! The kisses at his neck and the fingers in his ass put paid to that thought, thoughts of anything, the one that he should think of more. Should he stop this? Oh, but he wanted to so very much.

But didn't.

"Mine," Fess muttered, and Deacon felt fingers in his ass being placed by a... thick, bulbous throbbing cock. That nudged at his tight entrance with a sense of urgency. As thick as his manly wrist.

Now he was the one who groaned aloud at the prod, prod of the waiting penis at his ass entrance. He could hear Fess chuckle.

"Yours." Deacon agreed on turning and seeing the possessive look that fleeted across Fess. Eyes of fire and flame.

"I have never done this before..."

An admission that was unexpected from the weird though enticing man's lips.

What? Never? How could this be? With women or with men? Deacon stilled for a moment as he processed what this admission could possibly mean. He did not want to be someone's fuck toy. Then left once used to go find another. A gay experiment.

"Never?" Deacon moaned aloud as the large feeling; thick cock continued to nudge his entrance without delving in fully to it.

Only the tip had taken ownership there. Sliding around. Teasing him. Feeling him.

"Mmm," Fess replied as he nibbled Deacon's neck. He seemed to have a thing for it…licking right where the vein of his neck would be, "Never…" He panted in answer, "With a man…"

"Oh." Said Deacon stunned. So that was what he had meant. This god-appearing man had never been with a man before? Not ever…the thought thrilled him. Worried him.

He was the first and… he did not know whether to be relieved by this or worried that for Fess it could end up being a mistake as like what had only just crossed his mind moments before. Deacon had met a man before who was confused about his sexuality.

Toing and froing, messing him about. Still fucking women and really secretly wanting men.

But how could something this bloody good, this right, this final be a mistake? Trying though to block out the ugly, so ugly burns that raced down the sex god's body in a layer of zig zags as he turned.

The ones that Fess was iffy about receiving.

No normal person would be burned alive like that and just hanging around taking random men to bed with them as if it was an everyday occurrence. Or be in the mood to.

They would be in the hospital, surely? Especially with marks that ran that deep. Fess was clearly no ordinary man though. Deacon could tell.

He was not sure about it. He was perfect apart from them. Could he forget them? He would try to. Perfection was just a part of his person so maybe he needed some imperfection into his world for a bit of balance.

"Do you want to stop?" Deacon added tensing up.

Fess licked his neck.

Moaning. Enjoying the flavour it seemed.

Hoping to god that Fess said no. Please say no, his body yearned for the cock that wanted to break down its gentle barrier.

Which it did.

"No. Never!" Fess demanded. Running his hand through his human`s hair while the other one took hold of his demanding hips.

"All right then…"

"Do you need lube, my mortal?"

Deacon had sworn that he had said mortal. But no, it must have been something else that he had said. What sounded like mortal?

That – he did not know. His lust dazed mind too swept up to care.

Deacon smiled warmly, "I would usually, but I am that fucking horny that as of now I need none…"

"Don't say I didn't warn you then…" Almost roaring as Fess now plunged his throbbing cock deep and hard right into where it most belonged to be in.

With the person that was destined for him in every way that was possible. He would not have his heart – he did not deserve it in any shape or form.

Fess knew that. He owned it.

But he would have the humans body and mind. They were meant for him and him alone. He would see to that.

Fess thrust deep into his soul mate's firm ass without any further delay.

This should feel wrong. His cock in another man. He should feel shame as he had never done this before, never thought about it before, never expected it, but found that he – didn't, feeling only sensations and joy.

Pleasure. Hope.

He gently spanked the curvy ass with the palm of a hand as he continued to plunge harder and harder right from the back. Enjoying the grunts and moans that left his human's sweet mouth, urging him for more. The mouth that one day soon would be choking on the edge of his impressive cock.

He would see to that.

The one that was currently been rammed home right there on the bed.

A bed that soon would be no more. His mate deserved better. Far better.

He would give him everything that he so wanted!

His mate was enjoying it anyway as he squirmed underneath Fess`s body. He would not hurt him.

He would kill anyone who tried to either. He might be scared of Rhys like he was the devil himself if he so existed, that man brought cool shivers down his spine, but that man was not touching his Deacon.

His human.

One day a Vampire eternal like he also. That was all he could be for their bond needed that to ignite.

Fess lightly touched Deacon`s cock as he murmured in sweet bliss. Never having touched a cock, but his own one. Smaller than his own one he found, but still it felt so good in his bare closed grip.

Slowly fisting it with his palm. Faster, faster. Speeding up with the whimpers.

Then after barely minutes of thrusting of both hand and cock, bringing his mate hard to climax, and then he also in return right after.

"Oh my god!"

As Fess came, his cum dripping from his human's bare tantalising bum, he made a fatal mistake.

A mistake that could be his undoing and one that he would regret for an eternity. Too overcome with hunger for his mate.

Hunger to mark him.

Then a hunger for his blood that cried out silently for him to feed from the gasping gentle human.

To try it. Wondering impatiently what it would taste like? Like a forbidden fruit or the finest wine? Almost drooling.

He bit down into Deacon's neck before his mind could betray him with his newly erupted fangs – and drank down hungrily.

It took a few moments for his human to realise that Fess wasn't having a playful bite of his slender neck – but was doing something else entirely.

Something unexpected…

"What? What the!" Deacon pulled away in horror that blighted his smooth, stunned face as it finally hit him head on what had just happened to him by another. Something that was like out of a budget movie or a cheesy book.

That he had just been fucked hard and taken to heaven and back by a vampire.

Bitten by one. Drank from.

One that no one else but he could see…

He was fucked. Literally…

CHAPTER FIVE

Deacon

How could he have been so stupid not to have realised that something was amiss here? He scolded himself for jumping in to things again. One to not think and just take the bull by the horns.

Or the cock...

As his slapped arse hole burned slightly from the total lack of lube that had been used thanks to him and his whole naked eagerness, and lots of instinct, too much instinct! That cock he was surprised even fit in there.

An impressive, vampire dick.

As the lust googles started to wear away he pulled quickly away from the dark blonde-haired hottie who could rip him into two, away from what he thought was a divine creature like nothing he had ever known before.

Realising now that instead of a naughty, sinful angel taking him there in his flat, he had just been fucked hard by a vampire until they had both come in a series of grunts and groans that shattered and sinned.

The world still spun.

And then he had been naughtily bitten, his precious blood had been taken by another without permission granted. His eyes grew wide as saucers as he turned around slowly, throbbing still.

Heart beating fast anxiously. Thump, thump, thump. It sounded like it might take off with how scared he now was. The risk that he had taken.

Fess stood there with a sharp frown, stark bollock naked in all his devilish, handsome glory. His large, thick cock hanging there like an impressive third leg that beckoned anyone to resist it.

No wonder Deacon ached deep inside as if it had hit his guts when it had taken aim.

Deacon's blood now dripped down a perfect smirking mouth which was unconsciously wiped away with a smug, sincere smile.

Licking tempting lips with a tantalising tongue as the metallic blood hit the taste buds.

He now had fangs and red eyes that glinted dangerously with a hint of a warning. Black, magnificent wings shot out once again.

One appeared to Deacon to be crooked.

Uneven.

Could vampires hypnotise he wondered uneasily? Made to obey his every whim. Was he about to be hypnotised to be this vamp`s sex slave for all eternity? Made to go on his hands and knees and take it when the moment took the other.

It could be worse.

Now he was hard again. Damn it!

But no, he needed out of there quickly or to get the vamp out before he changed his mind and gave in to him. He had taken his blood from him! Without consent and that was important. Everybody with a brain knew that!

Not knowing how much of the myths about the bloodsuckers were true, he could have laser beam eyes for all he knew! That would be handy…

"Your blood was delicious." An orgasmic-sounding groan again from the creature with the teeth like pliers.

"Shit, shit, shit!" Deacon uttered in a state of panic now. His desire long forgotten.

Realisation. They had not used protection at all in their haste to get the other one naked in bed as quick as could be.

Did vampires get STDs he wondered, studying him? He doubted it. Knowing his luck, they could. Might wake up with warts on his penis.

But fuck...

Deacon took in a deep breath, in, out, in, out and could feel himself being watched as he felt in the middle of a vast nervous breakdown. But the heat that had burned between them had now gone out like a blown light.

He knew what he was about to say before he said it,

"Deacon, I..." The vampire said.

"No," Deacon argued pushing back.

"It`s ok."

"It fucking well isn't!" A flustered wave of the arms. Gesturing that this was not even close to being normal.

"It is. Please." The vampire had now put his sharp teeth away and his eyes flickered to their usual yellowy-brown colour. The feeling at his fragile neck had been rather nice after a bit, but no, no, no! he did not want to be eaten alive by another.

Even if he was being bummed hard into ecstasy at the same time that he had lost his senses! "Breathe. Deep breaths. Be calm my little mortal one."

"Breathe… It's ok for you, I doubt you can do that."

"No." A sigh.

"Please, just get out." Deacon cried out in a panic. Fuck, he didn't even bloody breathe! How the fuck was he alive then? Or kind of alive…

Fess gave him a concerned look and dressed quickly without delay. Still in his monstrous form. The burns now thick and there.

Every detail accentuated. Claws sprang from nails that could take one's eyes out. The fangs and scarlet eyes returned as if he could not keep control of himself.

Tried to.

"Let me explain," Fess said gently. "Deacon…" He urged. Moving forward towards the frightened young human. An arm out to steady him.

Too close.

Not close enough.

Oh, Deacon did not know, his cock still throbbed eagerly as though it wanted more from the supernatural being, the one that scared him as well as intrigued him, and his ass was clearly spent for a time after the effort.

It had been good sex for a man virgin.

Too good.

Had that all been a lie to get him into bed? Get him naked and bent over in a compromising, erotic position? One that at the time he hadn't minded being bent in?

But fuck...a vampire had just taken a bite out of him. He could still feel the tingle from the fangs that had sunk into his blushed skin. Ones that still stuck out in the thick-lipped mouth that he so desperately wanted to kiss again.

Now he knew why... supernatural abilities... was he going to be for dinner? About to be eaten alive and his blood drained dry?

He had to get this vamp out of there.

Now.

And he still had to go to work in one piece.

He could not let anyone down that day... his clients needed him, the animals, and their pet parents besides.

"No, no!" Deacon heroically argued. Coming to his senses.

Trying to anyway.

"Deacon, listen. Yes, I am a vampire. Yes, only you and other vampires what not, can see me. But I will never hurt you. I swear. Never!" Fess roared right near him like a lion possessed. Grabbing onto Deacon, gripping his arm and clearly not letting go any time soon.

Only calmed by his presence.

Putting a raised palm to the human chest, then thus hearing the throb of his mate's panicked heart.

Stilling. He appeared ashamed of his actions. His mate's vulnerability was apparent. His weakness.

"Do you have a heartbeat, Fess? Though I suppose if you do not breathe then that answers my question doesn't it?" Deacon said as his own one pound pounded against the clawed hand that was still gentle, although the claws were so sharp that he could likely rip out his heart with them if he so wanted to.

"No...no, I don't sadly. Not Anymore. But I did once. I wish I still did." Fess paused on the spot as if frozen into place, and his face returned to human-like again much to Deacon's relief and he pulled away from the only hard chest that still beat. The claws returned to human nails.

"But I still feel Deacon, my god, I still feel. And now I feel more!" His entire gaze bore into the humans.

Unwavering. Like he dared him to look away.

"No, you don't. How could you, Fess? Feeling is a human trait."

"Yes, I do." A shimmer flickered in his vampire eyes. "I feel everything when I am with you. Nothing when I am not. You were all I thought after the last time that we met. You were what got me through the flames as I screamed in pain."

Deacon edged forward as if to touch Fess`s smooth covered chest, looking as if he wanted to jump right into his sweet-ass moulded firm arms, but seemed too scared to.

So, he didn't.

"Why can I see you, but no one else can?" The intrigued human asked the invisible vampire curiously. The one who had a hard shell, but inside there was something softer.

Fess grimaced obviously not wanting to be dragged into it all any further, "It's complicated...Deacon, you should go to work now. Time is ticking. I can leave by the time you return here this evening if you want me to. Maybe it is for the best. I would never hurt you and you have to believe me with every fibre of my being. But others might do to get to me. The one that burned me could. He is crazier than a box of frogs. I could not risk it; I could not abide it." The blonde spat out with rage aimed at another but he.

Deacon frowned, feeling apparent unease at the thought of a mad vamp being after either one of them. One that could cause an extreme amount of harm -especially himself because he was just human, and Fess had obviously already come up a cropper when faced with the psycho vamp as one also. So, what chance did he as a simple, nature-loving human have?

None. Precisely that.

Zero.

And would he, Deacon wondered be able to see the maddened vamp with his own bare eyes if he looked for him? He did not know the ins and the outs about what he would see and what he would not be able to, but it bothered him either way that he only knew a fraction of what could await him.

Blocking it out for a time he grabbed his work clothes together and got quickly dressed in a flurry of clothes. Eying the pile of laundry that was stacking up from the weekend. Cursing the need for a coffee that went through him as he eyed his messy kitchen. That was if he could find a cup. A nice warming drink that would help him think. He needed to!

Thinking also with regret that he had been a bad host and not even offered his guest one.

But he had had a drink. Of him…was that even enough? Did vampires drink normal liquids?

It better have been enough. There would be no second chances if there even were one… the sudden bite to the neck had nearly given him a heart attack.

"I need time to think." He said to the waiting vamp who just nodded.

Tension wild in the air.

The vamp seemed not to be deterred and carried on regardless, "Fair play. You work at a veterinary practice I see?" Fess asked with interest seeing the logo on his man's top there for all to see.

Looking proud of it as he smiled for a change. Deacon thought he looked so good when he smiled with genuine warmth that radiated off of him.

Sitting down on a chair at the side of the room and draping himself about with relative ease as if it were his own home now.

Scanning the human up and down.

Where did he live? Deacon did not know this.

Fess stared at his neck eagerly. Likely remembering the illicit blood that had tasted like something out of an amazing fairy tale.

"Yes." Deacon snapped and brushed down his top. But then curiosity got the better of him, his head looked up, "What did you used to do then?"

"Used to!" Fess chuckled. "Am I that washed up that I just spend my day as a deceased, blood-drinking corpse?!"

"No…"

Another blush. That brought on a predatory look from Fess. The blonde vampire, "I have never laughed so much since meeting you, my little mortal man. You human will be the real death of me if you carry on with this endearing, innocent way." He jibbed.

Ways that Fess looked like he could think a thousand times of corrupting.

He seemed the sort to like a challenge.

"For a vampire, you say the nicest of things. I don't think you are as bad as you want me to think." Except in the bedroom. Bad to the bone.

"You sure? I thought you were shit scared of me. I thought you wanted me out?" Fess grinned in reply. Licking his lips.

"I do. I did…I don't know!" An exasperated sigh with unspoken words from an exasperated human mate.

Fess said with a warm twinkle in his eyes, "I was into cars. Big time. I was a mechanic although it was not that job that killed me in the end. Now I am a soul collector for a higher being, It is why vampires were created in the first instance. Although now with my burns and my wings and everything else stopping me from doing my eternal job, then I doubt I am able to continue on. I will possibly be wiped out as I am of no use to continue what I was saved for…"

Deacon shuddered, "I am sorry. I didn't mean…"

"Don't apologise my little mortal. Now go. I will let myself out." Fess waved a hand.

"Why do you call me yours? How do you know this?" An eager look that nearly made Fess look as if he wanted to take his human right up there against the living room wall.

Deacon could be persuaded. You bet you!

"Because you are." Fact.

"But how do you know this Fess? You did not answer me, and I feel like there is more that I am yet to know." Unaware that he had nearly hit the nail on the head.

Fess strode over and took ownership of his quaking man. His lovely one. Gripping him tight.

"It is what we were destined to be. Can you not feel the pull right there between us my sweet darling, Deacon?" He growled. "It will stay that way forever. Until my immortality ends. There is no un - connecting us."

"I do. I feel it. I feel you." Deacon's face filled with a wide smile. Like all his wildest dreams had come to a reality.

Fess took him into his hold and gave him a hard lingering kiss. Working his way then to the neck that had tasted so good before.

It would do again.

Deacon flinched. His eyes nearly bulged out of the sockets.

Fess teased, "I crave you. In every way that is possible. But I won't do it again. Not until you beg for it. Then I will take it eagerly." Licking his perfect lips.

"Thank you." A sad deflated sigh.

"You won't be when I am going through blood lust, and you have to chain me up to prevent me from simply taking it." Eyebrows shot to the sky. A hidden innuendo that made Deacon thirsty for more.

And he wasn't the vampire.

"If you do not get it from me where would you usually get it?" he asked. Hoping that the vamp did not just go around sucking other men. Only he wanted those lips around his. Those fangs there at his neck.

"Do you really want to know?"

"Mmm." A simple nod. For he did.

So, Fess began, and Deacon listened to him eagerly, for the blonde one beside him was rather interesting.

Wise.

"This is for your ears only. No one else must know. I do not know what will happen if others find out, but it has been a kept secret for many thousands of years. Understand?"

"Yes. Of course. Who would believe me anyway?" Deacon asked.

"Oh, I don't know. Some whacky person out there. I know there have started to be rumours about invisible beings snatching people, I cannot afford to let the flames be stoked."

"Understood. I wouldn't have believed it until I saw it for myself. Most people wouldn't." A smile.

"But they could. And where would we then be? The reasons vampires were first created back when is we are soul collectors. We take souls to the judgment realm then the soul is sent onto your version of heaven or hell. This part after we have no opinion on.

"Wow…"

"Before we take the recently departed one away, we can drain the blood of the soul's body before they go on for their final judgment elsewhere. Also, we have been known to bite unsuspecting humans, although I tend to go for just the bad ones. A stalker or two, a killer or three. Ever heard of a wanted person going on the run and never to be seen again?

"Sometimes..." Deacons eyes flashed nervously.

"I normally feast on them. That is why they are never seen again."

"Oh. This is a lot to process, Fess. I should go to work."

"Of course."

"But, how long before. You know..."

Fess chuckled. "Need to feed? Ages. We can survive without blood although it can make us incredibly weak without it. More likely to get blood lust..."

His human evidently did not like the sound of that.

Blood lust. He did not have to ask what they were.

It was obvious. He would have to think of their next move.

For he would need blood. He could not deny him that. He should.

He still could not.

"Although after tasting yours it would be rather like having a burger once I had had some steak to eat-the finest. I can still taste it lingering in my senses. I am sorry, but I find I am also not."

Deacon with his face flaming shot out of there at the speed of light, almost forgetting his keys in the process. Begrudgingly heading back inside for his phone, his black jacket, and his kit. But not before stopping and saying to the crazed vampire, house guest in a quiet, sweet voice that melted his darkened soul.

Brought in the light that it had not seen in a long time - if at ever. Who was currently making himself at home in his flat, putting the kettle on.

Seemingly human everyday things. But this was no human there, this was someone that Deacon had to watch. But also, someone that he remained tied to somehow. He would feel relief if he got back, and Fess had gone from there. Never to be seen by even him again.

But also, sadness.

Sadness like no other. He would pine for him. Think of him when spread-eagled while with another male. If he could bear to lay with one.

"I hope that you are not wiped out, Fess."

Then with a spring in his smiling self, a typical morning person - he left his home. Leaving the vampire alone in his home - speechless.

CHAPTER SIX

<u>Fess</u>

His delicious enticing human left in a fleeting dash as he gazed back after him with forbidden interest. The past few hours flitted through him as though he were still reliving them minute by minute.

Oh, they would re-live them all right. Together night after night until the sun started to rise over the night sky and a new day would begin.

Vampires could walk in the sun – another myth made by humans.

Whether he had to chain his human to the ground to make him his for all of eternity and more if he was able, to stay with him, to keep him - he would do it.

He had a feeling that this was not the case here though with this awkward man of his. The one who with a glance he knew that he had been through unmentionable things.

Knowing that he could order the sweet human to his knees without a shred of clothing, and he knew they would obey the eternal one willingly regardless.

That he would take him for exactly who he was and accept him. Vampire and all.

Every time.

The fabulous first-time sex with someone of the same sex, the kissing, groping, the sex. Oh, the sex…it was so worth it.

He felt like he had died again and gone to the higher plains when he had placed his large hands on his tantalising man.

Sighing with a strange feeling of contentment.

Never having felt that before and hoping that it stayed with him forever.

But it was not just that frantic lovemaking, that had made Fess decide to stay there in that ratty apartment in the city, in the search of caffeine and some passable food to eat.

Not then once the little vet nurse had left after coming backwards and forwards, backwards and forwards because he had forgotten everything and had to return back there.

He just wanted to.

It felt right to be there with his fragile human. This was his place here. And…and he was kinda banished from most places now, so he had no other option but to stay close…to keep his other part safe.

He belonged with this human.

His Deacon.

Even if the fated bond didn't link them thus he would still be obsessed with him and to feel his own state of vampiric giddiness on thinking of him.

Fess graciously went off for another coffee from the cluttered kitchen. Unwashed cups, cutlery, and a greasy sink full of washing up that irked him. A kitchen that brought out a sigh of frustration at its sheer grottiness.

"Deacon, Deacon, Deacon," He sighed. "What will we do with you eh?"

Oh, he knew…

Food in the fridge that was the kind that a dieting rabbit would eat. He could tell his little vet nurse was a health freak.

Oh dear.

He himself preferred a fry-up or a nice, juicy fat burger.

There was none of that in here…his poor mate. Look at what he was missing out on by eating all this healthy shit that no one in their right mind would want to eat, but him!

Fess would for sure not be wasting an eternity alive eating salads, protein bars and what not that tasted of plastic.

He hungered for meat, for blood. For his new man...

And now for something that he had only just come to crave.

That perfect-sized cock that had dangled between Deacon's legs naughtily as he accepted his own one in his un-lubed hole. He wondered how many other men had been there in that warm flesh hole.

The thought did not appeal to him.

Jealousy threatened to rear its unfriendly head.

Bringing the hot drink to his lips that tasted superb he threw himself onto the messy bed, turning on the nearby TV with a tattered remote.

Searching for trashy TV, something to pass the time with.

The drink that met his lips was not as superb tasting as the moreish stream that had left his mate's neck with temptation behind it, although it was still nice.

Mate though.

He had a mate. An actual fated one for him and him alone who no one else could dare touch - but him. Never in his ten years walking the realms alone barr a few friends who had mainly disowned him, had he expected to have one for his very own.

Wiping the sweat away.

He did not know if Deacon realised they were said mates though. Had not taken the time to divulge this piece of info except to say it basically.

One day he would.

He would have to see to that. Guarantee that.

He after being fed, just, and his thirst quenched had a brief nap, full and content with a fanged smile on his handsome, chiselled face and then cleaned his little mortals home until it was sparkling.

Enjoying the humanity feeling that these simple chores brought to him. Scrubbing the kitchen, putting the Hoover round and the ragged mop.

If only the vampires could see him here now. But they wouldn't. Couldn't. Plus, he found that he didn't care anymore.

Running a bubble bath, he pulled himself gently into it as the bubbles grew and the water rose high.

Just as Fess began to succumb to the soothing lull of the bath that drew him into its pleasurable bliss, the abrupt sound of the doorbell jolted him awake from his doze. He had been examining the tapestry of scars, burns, and marks that adorned his inhuman skin, a silent testament to his recent past. "Who on earth could that be?" he mused; his tranquillity now brutally disrupted by another. He had not expected anyone to interrupt him.

Swiftly, he rose from the now sadly abandoned bath, water droplets cascading down his glorious, rugged form. He reached for a nearby clean towel, drying himself off before slipping into a borrowed navy t-shirt that hung from a hanger a similar size to he, and also a pair of black short-like pants that hugged his muscled curves.

A hint of cheek showing.

It was his man's shirt, a comforting reminder of their bond as he sniffed it.

Unwashed.

It still smelled of him if he lifted his nose to it. A hint of musk and a fragrance of lynx. He was not sure which one, but it was the one he was wearing earlier.

When Fess had lost his cool and bitten into something that he shouldn't have. Something that was so incredibly sweet.

With a sense of curiosity, he moved towards the nearby back window, peering through a crack in the curtains to see if he could see who it was that dared to disturb him from his dream-filled bath time in his mates flat.

His eyes narrowed in sourness, trying to discern the figure that stood at the door.

Not sure who they were. Of course, he would not know who they were, he did not live there – yet. That was in the future, and this was the now.

But if Deacon would have him, then he would follow him to the ends of the earth – if he let him that were. He had not been sure how he felt at first about being destined to a man. Entwined for all eternity.

Two cocks, one bed.

Now he knew it was what always had laid there hidden in his very darkened soul.

Only Deacon had been the one with the key to unlock it and unleash it to the world. The one to embrace him. Embrace it.

He could still feel his sweet lips reciprocating his, his gentle moans, and the tongue of his mate that gently probed for more.

Super protective of his new mate. Red tinged his eyes as the door went yet again causing fury. Ignoring it hadn't given the person the message that no one was in.

And he was fucking invisible, damn it! How was he supposed to answer the bloody door anyway? They wouldn't bloody see him!

Nor did he really want to. When this was all over he would see to it that Deacon lived elsewhere but there with one of those fancy ring doorbells that he knew these humans liked. Somewhere better. Cleaner.

Meat in the fridge and cake in the cupboards. Salad if he must.

A warm, clean home to come to after a hard day with unruly animals. Followed by hard, nights.

Naked ones covered in oil.

The doorbell was held down and so it rang and rang – and rang. If he had a heart that still beat like a human one did then it would have thudded a series of beats as the doorbell rang constantly as if the caller had fallen down dead upon pressing upon it.

Causing a strange sense of anxiousness to unnerve him.

It was an older man at the door he could see. Roughly mid-fifties. Serious looking -sour. He had a smart, expensive tailored suit on which still didn't make him look any better and polished shoes to match. Gelled back hair and a snide expression.

He gave Fess the creeps he found. And not many people did that as Fess was – immortal. He could snap this man in two and drain him dry in the blink of an eye before the beady-eyed man knew what had hit him. After all, he was an invisible threat, a hidden predator.

A pissed off, interrupted one.

Fess could do what he liked with the man and only one of them would live to tell the tale.

But look where that had got him before... he wouldn't though, in case the older gent, but not quite a gent meant something to his sweet, dear mortal.

The one who he wanted to devour again later. So hard that he wouldn't feel his own ass even if he was sat upon it. He bet that he would enjoy it just as much as he would. Would he let him return the favour?

Let the human thrust his cock up his own virgin arse?

He was not quite sure yet.

For Rome was not built in a day, was it? They had all the time in the world, the realms, to work things out about who took who and where. It would start with the auburn-headed one.

Not red, not ginger or carrot – auburn. He would be taken and thank him for it later.

Fuck! Fess nearly turned around and got back into bed for a wank. Although he wanted – no needed, to see who this creepy man at the door was. Couldn't rip down his boxers and stroke himself into sweet fine oblivion whilst a stranger was calling.

For his fated mate...growl.

He needed to take action.

"You had better be a relative." He muttered with displeasure as he scoured the stranger up and down again through the gap where he currently stood lurking. Seething with pent-up anger at someone that he did not know.

But then he heard it.

The man had walked away from the door in long, thin strides and was now talking to an older woman next door with bushy hair and thick brows, but an endearing face as if she had lived an enchanting life.

The only bonus of Deacon living in a grot pit with thin walls and no insulation. Fess could hear everything.

The man asking her about Deacon. Said he was his dad.

Oh. Dad?

Deacon had not mentioned him to him so far although so far they had not had the time to talk more in-depth about family, work, and any friendships that they both had. As he watched being invisible to all around except for one who was not there, though he should be, the grungy man moved over to speak to the woman closer, Fess slipped around the front way and left through the door.

Darting back to the back path again – to listen in more eagerly.

Now he awaited for further intel patiently.

Ok, impatiently…

The neighbour said in response to the dominating man warily, "He is at work at the moment. I saw him leave here not long ago. Such a sweet boy. You must be so proud of him being your son." She smiled fondly at the mention of sweet, innocent Deacon.

Hmm, Fess thought.

If only she had seen that sweet boy being ploughed hard from behind while his nuts swung to, and his cock throbbed with pre cum earlier! Would she say he was sweet then?

He doubted it.

That was an image only Fess had permission to see. He would not share his new man with anyone. The one sent for him and him alone.

For all vampires treasured their mates like diamonds.

For it was destiny. And he guessed Deacon was his.

Man, and all. Wary of his scars and all – for he had seen his wrinkled in disgust on seeing them.

"Where?" The man asked her roughly glowering. Pulling himself self-up to full height over the small, crooked fence. The only thing that stood between them. Just.

A typical overbearing male.

Much like Rhys, except not as handsome and not as old. And a lot less powerful…"Where does my boy work?" A horrible sneer that made him look rotten. Not a question with worry ,but one of something that were hidden dark.

Deep.

The sweet old lady seemed taken aback by this urgent demand at her fence when she had Fess guessed, merely been putting her washing out on the line. A ghastly assortment of big knickers in an array of colours and flowery dresses that one would need sunglasses to look at for too long.

A fear of fright flickered on her face which she quickly seemed to will away as she gathered her braveness, "I don't know." Fess could sniff out a lie a mile away on anyone and he edged closer in case he had to protect the feeble woman from this frightful man.

For he would.

An invisible hero with fists clenched at his sides in outrage. She distrusted this man here. He could sense it from a mile away. The sullen stranger at his mate's door who oozed venom beneath his smart suit. Fess would nick the best box of chocolates that he could find – and leave them at the elderly woman's door.

Yep, going soft…

The man, dad, probed, "You must. You know him don't you?"

The lady huffed, "If he is your son then surely you would know where he works. Wouldn't you? Know how he was. I'm just a neighbour minding my own. Now I have things to do, and I can't stop and talk all day."

The man nodded then still had something that he seemed to want to say. "Is he still…?" Silent words with a hidden meaning.

"Still?" She frowned in confusion as she made to leave.

The man sneered, "You know. Into those that he shouldn't be?"

"Like?"

" Men." He spat with a look of scorn on his unpleasant face. Fess`s claws made purple blood ooze from his palms as they dug in in his outrage.

Oh, hell naw! What the actual fuckety fuck! What was this guy on about? What century was he in? This was 2024 after all and not the olden days.

The woman seemed to thankfully be horrified by all this and after muttering that it wasn't simply her business she un - merrily marched into the house and shut the door quickly to. Looking as if she could have then it would have been in the man's face.

Fess had to stop himself from ripping the guy's throat out there and then on the spot and throwing his corpse onto the stones on the ground next to the flat. The ones that crunched underfoot so he had to be quiet when he trod.

Unseen, but not unheard.

Dad! What the heck!

A lousy one at that. His own one thought that he was dead. This one knew that his son was alive and well, walking around with a blissful fucked smile on his face and a sore ass, he did regret that one, and still thought that little of him that he dissed who he truly was to all and sundry.

At his door.

Didn't care who he could truly be.

All because of his son's sexual identity! The one that had nothing to do with anybody, but him.

Fess could kill him. He really could. But death did not deserve him.

He wanted to so fucking badly that he would give up his immortality to! Claws shot out on his bare hands, and he stifled a menacing growl. But something stopped him as he did so. A small voice in the back of his head urged him to think of the human.

Again.

Should he, he wondered? It was like having a devil perching there on one shoulder and an angel lingering around on the other one. Urging him to be good.

Telling him to be bad.

But he didn't want to be bad anymore. The thought of Deacon and his eyes aflame with anger at him as he had done something to upset him made something surge in his chest. The man deserved his comeuppance. One day.

And anyway, how come Deacon didn't see him anymore? Was it because his dad was an ass?

Probably. The man did not deserve a glorious son just like Deacon.

He deserved a son-in-law just like Fess though. One who if he could see him, know him, would have made his every day a living nightmare until the day the miserable fucker drew his last breath…

Dearest, daddy dickhead, walked past Fess whose skin bristled as they accidentally touched each other faintly. The man stopped all of a sudden and frowned deeply.

Giving Fess the chance - to push him right over.

Hard.

"Hey, what the fuck!" The man groaned as he fell like a stack of cards, cutting his hands on the sharp stones, on the bare ground.

Fess quietly sniggered in merriment.

Enjoying the show. Enjoying every second of seeing the gelled-haired man on his knees on the ground. His victim rose again and looked around to search for who had dared to attack him.

But he would never see them.

Shaking his head and thus so carried on his way out of there.

Fess grabbed him again without any delay.

Kicking him in each knee, causing the man to screech in pain, clutching his knees with hairy, thick fingers splayed while Fess, laughed gently to himself at the sight before him. Eyes twinkling in amusement.

Tears running down his cheek. In his eyes that man had asked for all of that.

He deserved far, far more besides.

He could smell the blood as if it was throbbing right through him.

Good. That must mean he had made that stupid, cretin bleed.

Thinking again. No, Fess no. You are not tasting his blood. When his son`s is far finer…

Ten years back and the newly turned Fess who had been saved from an eternal slumber, would have struggled at the smell of blood that lingered there in the air. That was dripping down the man's, dirty knee.

He was lucky. Today that man was lucky.

Not realising that he had been that close to a monster. And survived…

"Don't come back." He said brazenly into the man's ear with a rough whisper as his victim scabbled up in sheer fright. His whole demeanour changm. Laughing again as the man ran faster than his long trousered legs would carry him off into the city streets and away.

Now with that, as he watched the man flee, Fess was going to have to pay a visit.

To the vets.

Not someplace that he had ever envisioned himself needing to be… But now he did.

Not to see the animals, no. But the human who called out to his mind, his body and his once beating heart.

CHAPTER SEVEN

<u>Ten years ago.</u>

<u>Death day</u>

<u>Fess</u>

He awoke with a muddled mind filled with burning sins.
Groaning as his head felt like he had the world's worst
hangover. His limbs were heavy and there was a weird pain
in his back that zapped right through.
 Like something wanted to sprout out from it.
Burning.
Yep, he had drunk far too much that very night …
Earlier that night he had fallen into the city's river on a
drunken night out with his then girlfriend Elfina. Wanting to
look at the view in drunken awe at it, doing stupid things
like drunks can do without any thought, and to stop and
collect his thoughts when he had stumbled on his new shoes.
Designer don't you know.
Even them brand spanking new squeaky shoes couldn't save
him when the water grabbed him in its liquid grasp and

pulled him right in. He began panicking with fear as he hit the water, flailing his arms in the air, and yelling sweet curses to himself.

Swearing inside that he hadn't told anyone where he had now gone.

And drowning - a horrible death for anyone, not even he deserved that...

Praying that the bar that they were in would have working cameras to show where he had then gone.

This was Norfolk after all...

He managed to get swept away. When he thought that all hope was lost, when he thought that death was calling his name, the flowing water in the fearsome river stopped at an angle so he managed to get out in time before the water filled his lungs.

Drenched from head to toe he stupidly decided to make those who were looking for him wait to see his fate.

Fuck them, they could wait to see where his fate lay! Elfina - his girlfriend could wait. He had thought that they were good together, but with a sink of the stomach, he now thus thought otherwise.

Something was missing between them that he had not envisioned not being there. Something that he could not quite put his finger on.

Their sex life had died an unrecoverable death, and it couldn't be found which was unusual for people of their age. He could see with a saddened heart that she was looking elsewhere, wanting to be elsewhere minus him.

With someone else.

And Fess well… he would admit that he loved attention. Wanted to be noticed by all. And if that made him a drama queen - then so be it…

Not knowing as his drunken mind ticked along whether he wanted to pretend he was dead to them all or to start afresh after he fell into the freezing, rushing water.

Staggering still, having lost his new shoes in the depths of the water, had left the cold, cold water and clambered into his car that was parked half a mile down and left the city where he lived.

Unsure how he had got there.

Shivering cold, still pissed as a newt, he got quickly into his car and did one thing that he had never done before or thought that he ever would – he drunk drove home.

He didn't know what he was thinking, he would regret it for all of eternity. Forever more.

He didn't know how he came to reach that point in time where he had chosen to do something so dire that he could have hurt another person.

An innocent. But there he was, and the choice was now made.

He remembered the truck coming out of nowhere and a screech of its breaks. Not his as he was far, far, too drunk to have any reflexes in order to stop his vehicle in time.

His neck had swung back hard.

He had hit his head on the steering wheel with a clank, not feeling the airbags go off. Did they go off?

The next moment he was out stone cold.

The sound of help coming his way. "Hello, hello? Are you ok mate?"

But it was too late.

He had breathed his last. There would be no return and it was all his drunken fault.

"Where am I?" he groaned in a state of delirium. Unaware of his surroundings. Strange surroundings.

A man firmly tapped him on the shoulder and Fess spun around to see who was there.

Still confused.

Dazed. For he was not in his car where he should have been.

Not in a wreck trapped under a truck. Crumpled.

Or a hospital.

Oh, the walls were sparkling white, clean like a hospital was, but instead of medical care that one would bring it was like something he imagined Olympus looking like, where the gods were painted to have resided in back when.

Tall pillars, statues. Large, beautiful windows.

Awe inspiring.

A room filled with chairs…lots of them as far as the eye could see. Desks, people milling around busily. Some with fangs. Fangs! Some were just floating in mid-air. Ghosts?

No - souls.

Dwarfs lingering behind desks…beautiful, handsome ones, as though the confused Fess had plummeted straight into a fairy tale version of snow bite. Half expecting to see the Disney princess pop out for a brew and a chat.

The most handsome man that he had ever seen was the one tapping him on his shoulder. A man that looking back should have unveiled his bisexual lust, but it hadn't. Shaggy dark brown hair which flicked over his startling eyes, large broad shoulders as though he came with an axe as an extra.

And wings. Wings? What the…things were getting eerie.
Fess pointed at the wings that were far too life-like to be
anything else, but real.

Like the wings of a magnificent bird except firmer
appearing.

Larger. Magnificent.

His finger he glanced at. He was whole and not a ghost much
like some in the room seemed to be who were busy floating
around. He tried to breathe a sigh of relief, tried to exhale,
inhale, but found he couldn't do either…

The whole place was just simply unworldly. He felt
unworldly. Not normal.

Was he asleep? In a coma perhaps? Something else…his
heart should be beating a mile a minute through the fear that
he felt right then as his head whipped around the room
taking it all in.

But - nothing.

He felt cold touch his now pale skin as he splayed his hand
out.

"Is this a joke?"

He asked the godlike man for everyone else seemed busy,
who scrunched his nose up in concern that he might be on
the verge of a nervous breakdown.

Which he nearly was.

Taller than he the divine chiselled man looked down at Fess as though he was an innocent sweet child. Taking baby steps. No longer staggering, in pain, drunk, he felt only extreme hunger…

The man spoke in a mesmerising voice, "No, my friend. I am Iden - your sire. I saved you after the crash that killed you, made you like me. This is a lot to take in I know this. I have been in your position myself."

"Your sire…" That seemed familiar he had heard it said somewhere before… then it twigged quite where he had – "Oh, my bloody god! Sire! Am I dead?" A shocked dramatic gasp. Or something resembling one.

"Unfortunately, yes. Tell me how you feel about this lad." The man asked like a trained councillor sent his way. How did he feel? How did he think he felt?

He felt freaked out!

As he stared into the angelic man's eyes they changed colour right in front of him from a brown to red, to stormy midnight black as though he held the night sky in his mere vision.

"How! Are you jesting me?" Fess asked with worry.

The man tutted. "No, the pain that you feel in your back is where your wings are beginning to form. Sit." He gestured to a nearby seat as Fess felt his back burning and grimaced. Of seats there were plenty, "The thirst you feel? That is blood thirst. Your eyes are red. A danger sign at first. We will get you nourishment soon when we reach our realm. Please do not try to eat the dwarves they do not take kindly to this."

"Realm? Blood? Drink? No," That is disgusting!"

Fess exclaimed as he wriggled and fought his own mind in the chair where he now sat. Half thinking that this was all a sign of madness when the other half began to finally accept it.

Claws left his hands, and his eyes burned. His teeth seemed to be growing in his mouth so that he tasted his own blood spilling.

Sire? He was a fucking vampire! If he wasn't dead then he would want to be already at the pain...

"What is your name?" The man casually asked.

"Fess. I want no part of this - whatever this is. My family, friends, and my girlfriend are all waiting for me..."

This Iden now slowly shook his head, "I am sorry that life is done now for you. We need to check you in here at one of the desks, if you don't then you won't become a fully-fledged vamp. I normally ask permission to turn someone, but you were so out of it. You looked like you needed a second chance. Now come." Gesturing towards the many desks.

He knew where he was coming if he was ever short of chairs…

"What will happen if I don't?" Fess said brattily.

A sharp frown appeared.

Iden whispered in his ear roughly, "They will put you down like a dog." Then a bright welcoming smile.

"What?" Horror filled his veins.

Wings suddenly shot out of Fess`s now burning back as he screamed at the intensity of it all.

Cursing.

Ruing the day that he had ever gotten into that god-forsaken car intoxicated, wet, – and drove it.

Now this eternity - as this thing, in this way was his punishment.

And he would see it through…

CHAPTER EIGHT

<u>Deacon – now.</u>

The walk to work was bloody interesting if he did say so himself. He was floating on thin air as he walked straight towards his place of work in the hectic morning of the city, his heart beating steadily as he now picked up the pace so he could grab a coffee there, walking on sunshine at the so sexy vamp back at his flat who had made his heart leap, and his cock the hardest that it had ever been before.

Was he still there, he thought to himself worried?

His heart thumped again, skipping a beat even. He had better be he silently fumed! Not knowing how he would take it if Fess had left him for good although he really shouldn't care.

For he did not have his number, he did not know where he lived.

There was something there burning between them although he did not yet know what it was.

The scars where the sexy blonde was burned.

The ones that he could not bear to look at for too long, he wished that the guy's skin was flawless like it used to be back then when they had first met.

Like it was that time in the alley when it was pale and glistened in the low light.

But there was no help wishing…he needed to let his perfection ideals go.

For life was not like that after all…and life wasn't perfect.

Was Deacon in danger from bad vamps and all that he could not see, from him? The one that called him his destiny, though also just his mate.

That hurt, it really did. To have something so fine pulled away.

He didn't want to be just mates with him. Blatantly friend-zoned by a vamp.

But good enough to fuck, wasn't he? Would the vamp simply move on and fuck another?

The thought made him breathless. It hurt.

No, Fess made him breathless…

Now at work and struggling to concentrate on his veterinary nurse work when his brain wanted to think about one thing and one thing only and to simply ignore the rest of the world completely. To block it out.

Fess.

A strange name. A strange guy, vamp whatever. So almighty fine… he sighed happily in his own little bubble.

It was like being a teenager again when even the slightest thing, the slightest touch by one's crush, could make it spring to life downstairs.

More than Fess.

How had he died, he wondered over and over?

How did he still live? It was all such a mystery. So many questions and not enough answers to them, not enough time. Not enough guts to ask them of him either.

"You ok, Deacon?"

Little Abbi his co - worker asked as she took in his more usual than normal quietness. He was never the loudest person in a room - no, but today he was even quieter than usual.

Small build, and plump she was the vet he loved to work with the most out of all his colleagues put together. She made him giggle at the most insanest of things and she was - oh so brilliant at her job and fierce as.

Helping him towards his goal of being a fully-fledged vet one day.

Everyone loved her. He loved her.

She could tame the wildest rabbits and settle the nastiest dog, one who could give Cujo a run for his money with a mouth full of drool.

A shame the same couldn`t be said for her and men.

Don't let her looks fool you, he would think as people thought that she was a soft touch who wouldn't bite back.

That was always the misconception with shorter, smaller, happy people.

She did not need backup; she was the backup!

"Hey, Abs. Well… I just have a lot on my mind." He said as he helped her prepare ready for the day ahead whilst clutching a coffee.

The usual.

"Same. Same." She smiled warmly. Eyes not meeting the smile though.

"Justin?" He asked her daringly.

An on-off boyfriend who was not good enough for her in Deacon's opinion, was the only one that she was not fierce with, could be herself with and who would likely be the reason behind the vet's annoyance of the day.

Morning.

As he was every day.

 But there again he could talk. A hypocrite through and through.

For he was in lust with a vampire. What did he know about love? Nothing. He had never experienced it, not even close. She nodded.

 Oh, so it was Justin? Surprise, surprise!

Deacon bounded over clutching a new box of gloves, Abi had always said he reminded her of a Labrador puppy. He said she was a Rottie in return.

Eyeing her nervously, "I am in the same boat, Abs. I think that they are probably bad for me, the person that I like, but then again I am not too sure what is what."

He could slap himself.

"They...?" She pursed her lips and raised a wriggling brow in question. Silently probing him to reveal more than he was eager to.

Did he want to? He studied her. Looking at the white clinical door which was still thankfully closed to and decided to bravely answer his friend, slash colleague, "He." There he had said it.

Out loud. In the over eight years that he had worked there, he had always skirted around the issue. He gritted his teeth nervously.

Waiting for the evitable rejection for the fact that he was gay.

"I gathered." A warm reassuring smile. A tease.

"You knew all along? Do I scream gay or something?" He asked wiping a nervous brow.

"Haha no! You are just you, Deacon. How bad is he then?" An intrigued look. "Bad as in a bad boy or bad as in a hardened criminal. Is the sex good?" She probed nosily as friends do.

He just wished that he had confided in her.

"The first one. He has quite an important job. Not a criminal though."

"Oh, what is it?" Ears awaiting eagerly.

Fuck! He hadn't planned this at all, had he? Was just defending his man from anyone who may have a negative view of him. What the heck should he say now? He gulped.

"He delivers important things to places." Shuffling his legs, a thing that he had done since a kid every time that he had lied.

Like now.

"Oh! I wish Justin would get a job." She said.

"Me too!" She laughed at this honesty. For if your friends couldn't be honest with you who could?

"I am sorry that I didn't tell you, Abi. Hardly anyone knows. I have been bit before so –"

"Nonsense, Deacon, its fine!" Grinning at him with understanding.

They both turned their heads as the door seemed to then be pushed gently.

Then it shuddered to a stop.

"Strange," Abi said when no one appeared from behind it. Deacon had a funning feeling run through him as the door gently creaked again.

And there it was.

He was right like always.

Unless his tired eyes were deceiving him, Fess strode through the door – in his clothes, borrowed ones and looking hot as ever.

Droll worthy in fact… Abi spun around confused as the door creaked to.

Deacon just stood there with his gaping mouth open whilst Fess simply winked. Eyes blazing at the human in mad lust. Or he assumed it was this.

Stopping in front of him and waving cheerily in a sarcastic manner.

This invisible to some lark was just plain weird.

For he could see the dirty blonde male who blew him a cheeky kiss, who threw him a wink – she couldn't.

Would she ever or would it only be just he?

He expected not.

"We need to get this door looked at," Abi stated as she shut it firmly with an annoyed scowl at its creaking. Whilst the flexible Fess sprung quietly out of the way like an acrobatic rabbit.

Evidently used to being unseen.

Though felt.

Deacon wondered what it was like to be invisible to all others. He was not sure that he would like it even though he had no family that he would miss, only his work colleagues and friends.

It would be like being a ghost! Eerie.

"Hmm." Deacon was now lost for words. Head in the clouds. They had flown out of the window along with his dignity as his mouth dropped at the sudden intrusion.

His eyes caught Fess`s and took him in with a silent gaze.

Abi meanwhile clueless looked at her notes again for a refresh.

"Now, Pebbles the cat is back in."

"Again?" He whispered avoiding the vamp who was grinning at him wildly.

Pebbles.

The cat that might make him bleed just as much as the vampire had gone and done earlier. He hoped that the people hating cat, would behave in Fess`s presence – or god help them all. Fess seemed the protective sort.

"Yes, today is quite busy so get your head out of the clouds with your naughty lover boy." She marched over to the large walk-in cupboard and started fiddling with various things while Fess lurked straight over to Deacon like a predator on steroids.

He gasped. What!

Zoning in on his fragile prey with an arched brow the blonde vamp knew exactly what he was doing.

And who to.

The tread of steps lightly on the hard grey floor while he snuck, no leapt, to the frazzled vet nurse.

"Mmm." The watching vampire whispered running a hand down the flustered Deacon trying to obviously cop a quick feel and failing, as the human moved away each time the hand shot out to grab him.

Quietly with a growl, "Loverboy. More like my possession."

"Pack it in!" Deacon said as a scarlet blush hit his cheeks and he tried to get away from Fess, who clutched him firmly in his hold.

His vampire one.

Deacon could feel the sheer strength that came out in waves from the vampire's firmness.

He was drawing attention now, "Deacon? Everything ok there?" Abi pulled her head out of the large cupboard with a fluster of things in her grasp while Fess lightly chuckled at her under his breath, at her not being able to see him.

It clearly amused him in some way.

Likely still weird after all this time. "Can you hear laughing?" With a tilt of the head, Abi asked.

"Nah, probably just a pesky wasp or a bug making a noise." Deacon sniggered glancing at Fess who rolled his eyes at the hidden meaning. "If I see it I will swat it."

"Ew." She fiddled with her hair and put the items down near the main table. "This is a vet practice; you need to be an animal lover not go around murdering poor defenceless bugs." She joked. Then whispered, "I totally agree with you there. Bloody things…"

Fess growled at the closeness between the other two.

Abi jumped nearly ten feet in the air, "What was that? Weird."

"Just an annoyance."

Abi looked at Deacon oddly then glanced away. Turning to the door as the patient was due.

Precious, possibly evil - Pebbles.

Fess sidled over again to his squirming, annoyed human and after swatting said un-amused human on the bum, then went and sat in a nearby chair. To watch.

One of his favourite things to do apparently – to watch.

As he now appeared calm and collected.

Time whizzed by mainly smoothly and so after an hour or so of Fess being there, Deacon stopped worrying about him killing Abi, the animals, and possibly him, and began to relax in his job which he loved so fucking much.

Fess had only had one warning, an annoyed glare. So, when Abi abruptly left the room for her lunch break as the practise shut for lunch, while Deacon decided to sit and eat in the adjoining staff room for a change.

Alone. Or was he…? No, no he wasn't.

For as soon as the curvy vet had left and the rest of the staff too, Fess had followed him to the staff room, stuck his hands down Deacon's work uniform and coped a feel much to his delight, also possible annoyance.

"Pack it in!" Deacon had snapped slapping the groping hand away and glared at the grinning now-fanged vampire who was towered over him, licking his full delicious lips hungrily whilst trying - but failing, to get his wandering hands to strike gold.

Bingo!

"I nearly devoured her," Fess warned.

"She has a boyfriend. Stop being so jealous Fess, you said we are just friends and so just friends we will be."

"When?"

A fierce snarl echoed in the cream, cosy room and Deacon knew that he had made a bad mistake by this. He was then swiftly before he could breathe again lifted off the chair that he had been lounging in, and his healthy lunch fell to the ground with a sad splat.

"Oi!"

Fess after grimacing at the bland food there on the ground which he was glad that he was not the one who would be cleaning it up, spun the auburn-haired around and pulled him in for a lingering but rough stubbled kiss.

A kiss that would make one of them breathless, bring him to his knees and keep him there.

"You are fucking delicious! My human." A claim.

"Just stop with the – my human thing. It`s just…weird."

Fess pondered this for a moment, "But you are my human, D. Are you not?"

Deacon lowered his eyes. He was the first to pull away from the passionate embrace between them that felt like fire was filling the room.

Oh, how it burned…the desire between them. The vampires burning desire.

"You said, mates." He explained in a rush looking hurt by this.

Because he was.

He wanted more…so much more. The vamp before him may be dangerous, but he wanted to keep him.

Forever.

There could be nothing else, but them.

"Oh. For. Fucks. Sake." Fess`s face softened in realisation. "I will explain later I promise. On the walk home."

"Yeah?"

"Yes. Anyway, would friends do this? And I would try to act normal in case someone walks in. Then you will look fucking crackers, my salad, munching human."

Deacon smiled, "She has twenty minutes left, the rest longer, and she will never leave her lunch early. Probably meeting her stupid boyfriend."

"Hmmm. Sit down." Gesturing to a cosy chair.

Deacon sat down.

"I have never done this before." Another admission.

"Done what?"

Deacon soon had his answer and realised what Fess meant about acting completely normal. With a savage smile, he pushed Deacon back in the chair forcefully in surprise and unzipped the shocked man's flies slowly.

Teasing. Taunting. Tasting.

Deacon started to shake in anticipation at what was yet to come. Fess it seemed was coming more and more out of his comfort zone with him.

First sex with a man and now first oral with one.

A leap into the unknown- a leap onto something unexplained.

Deacon felt a strange buzz from that. Just with the movement of the zipper being pulled down, down and down furthermore, his firm pleasing, throbbing of course erection was immediate.

No arm up was needed. Fess would not let him have one anyway.

The devious Vampire got to his knees and got ready to put the humans delicious cock into his awaiting mouth with his eyes wide.

Seeming mesmerised by his first, thrusting cock.

"You sure?" Deacon asked gently.

"Positive."

A groan from the one there on their knees waiting to be fed the delicious meal of a human's thick cock. Acting submissive when he was the one who could simply whip his glorious wings out for show and tell and bleed the human dry right there in the office unnoticed by any others.

Deacon knew that by this act that Fess giving him the power over him that he doubted had been granted to any other.

He must think something of him.

If only that. If nothing more.

Fess roughly as if he was starving for food, starving for him - which he likely was, took the lengthening cock into his open mouth, trying to keep his fangs in check, trying not to bite and gently began to nibble on the oozing cock.

Dripping with pre cum for him.

Fess groaned as the salty taste hit his tongue. Gobbling it up eagerly like a good vamp whilst Deacon squirmed and cursed under his breath at how good it felt.

The kneeling blonde naughtily licked up and down the firm shaft, to begin with. Taking more and more of his awaiting man, his human, who was holding his breath in anticipation. One man had never been sucked off by a vampire, at work, and by one that no one else could see.

One that hungered for this fine dick as much as for his blood...

"Oh...Fess." A satisfied groan.

Deacon gently pushed the blonde-haired head down so that his cock was swallowed whole by the other. Enjoying the sensations that washed through him as his love took him in his mouth.

He could feel everything.

He did not need everything – just this! If he died he would die a happy man!

The mouth that encased him whole and gasped as he hit the back of the vampire's throat. Could feel every nook and cranny.

Fess gagged.

Not used to such a length, any length, in his fanged hungry mouth.

Who knew that Vampires had gag reflexes?

Deacon did now!

"Oh, are you choking on my dick, Vampire?" The human sniped. Playing the master when he knew that the one licking his length was as he groaned.

Fess nodded.

Mouth drooling. At least Deacon thought that Fess didn't have to worry about actually choking on it.

He was dead anyway!

As the curious Fess sucked, licked, and nibbled up and down his humans glorious cock and then gently took the balls into his mouth. Sucking. Choking on them.

Loving it.

"You were meant to suck my cock, you naughty boy."

Deacon piped up.

A nod again from the throat-filled one.

Well, an attempt of one as the meaty length hit the back of his throat again and again. Deacon could see the fanged one's erection through his black trousers.

Returning back to the neglected cock for a taste which without warning erupted into Fess`s mouth.

Taking him by surprise.

And Deacon.

"Fuccccck." Deacon had the orgasm to end orgasms as Fess tried to chug every passing drop down himself. A shudder as the sensations carried on and on - forever.

As he hoped he and the still-kneeling vamp would.

Deacon got up suddenly in panic as voices came from out in the reception, remembering now exactly where he was and so quickly zipped himself up as the room span with his glee.

Fess smiled, licking his lips which made his handsome features more striking to behold.

A proper dirty – blonde stud.

Deacon loved it when his man smiled. He worshiped him.

"Wait." Said Fess before Deacon pulled his trousers up too as well as the pants.

"Fess?" A longing whisper.

Pleading.

"I am still hungry."

"No more cock for you." Deacon felt that he was developing a kink. Fess too.

"Blood…" the vampire groaned as he sniffed, face changing in the afternoon sun that crept under the shut blinds.

"Will you be careful?" Deacon asked unsure.

"Yes."

"Someone is coming. It will have to be my neck again." A huff and puff.

"Please." Deacon pulled his clothes on and adjusted himself while Fess came over back in predator mode. Eyes on the delicate morsal.

Leaning in he was sniffed again.

"You like sniffing me." He noted.

"You smell good. You tasted it."

Deacon nearly came in his pants there and then. "Just get on with it! " he hissed as the noises rose.

Before he had even finished the sentence, Fess had stuck his fangs into the awaiting neck and was beginning his lunch time drink. Making satisfied groans as he wolfed his mate down like he had just done.

Deacon felt a pinch and then a strange sense of – bonding flow through him.

They were bonding.

Bonded even. He needed to feed him, his Fess, and look after him.

No, what was he doing?

"Are you hypnotising me?" Deacon said in an angry whisper.

"Don't believe all that shit!" Fess snarled. Pulling away from his humans neck. He was angry.

Very angry like a wounded bear. Hurt. "We don't hypnotise you numpty! Jeez. I will meet you outside at five o'clock. Oh, and if that dog in here ever hurts what is mine again then I will be having Mr Woof and his stinky ol blood for supper. Got it?"

 Snarling on edge.

Oh, there was snarling! Plenty of it.

"It`s an animal. He was in pain." Poor Mr Woof had a sore leg.

Fess rubbed his hands down his scars and gave an exasperated look. Deacon tried not to grimace.

"Don't care."

"Was it you who hissed at the cat earlier when it clawed me and Abi?

"Maybe." A shrug "Oh, and you have a hickey there." Nodding to his humans neck. "Might want to cover that up…" Fess grinned and then strode out of the room like a breeze.

The door slammed to.

Fucking vampires, Deacon cursed!

CHAPTER NINE

Fess

He leaned outside the packed vet having had to dodge and avoid all the various annoying people and took a minute out to collect his pacing thoughts. Wondering what to do in the four hours that he had left until his blushing mate finished his vital job.

He had hungered seeing the human filled with passion for his every day work. His mate deserved to be his own boss, in his own practice not under the rule of others. As long as he came home to him every day and not another, then he could have whatever the heck he liked from him!

Accessing his stash of money would be a different matter…

Four hours to be bored though so as he waited he spied the customers, the wandering people in the nearby streets and a variety of pets that casually passed through.

No, four hours to play.

Fess did not normally spend much time back in the human world apart from when during a most important soul call that was. During a soul call, he would go into a trance-like state and a message was relayed from somewhere that only he knew of.

He had to do his job, only a few circumstances excepted although he could pick and choose when he did it for the most part of it.

Most vampires after all were thankful for the work that they had been blessed to be given, the second chance of another life instead of being whisked off to the lower or higher plains for an eternity, and most vampires were not the dark deranged beasts that humans had guessed them to be.

Then after he departed to the human world to pick up the lost or nearly lost soul and had taken them to the judgment realm once he had filled up on their oh, so precious blood. Fess had had everything that he needed there in the vampire realm.

Not expecting that he would have a mate down below. Not thinking that he deserved one. Now he had to get used to the whole human like existence again.

Truth be told, Fess wouldn't hurt an animal unless he so had to. He was a vampire not a monster.

Growl – yes, scare – also yes if they hurt his man whom he was being oh so protective of.

Hurt – no.

The only cock that would be treated roughly by him was the one that he had just lovingly choked on. Exquisitely if he did say so himself - for his first time. Certainly not the last.

The thought of doing so before had not crossed his mind. He found with Deacon though that he had a range of firsts that he wanted to explore with this sweet human.

He would suck it again in a heartbeat – if he had one.

The moans and the groans that had slipped out of the surprised man's orgasmic mouth were as mind blowing as if it was his own dong that was being pleasured…

"I need a fag."

He sighed as it started to spit with rain. As he boredly glanced at someone nearby crouched on a bench with a Mars bar in one hand and a packet of fags in the other –not enjoying life. Blonde, hunched over and looking as though it was raining piss instead of mere water.

He was thinking about creeping over and taking one of those tempting fags into his mouth for it had been years since he had had a good smoke, but the mood just suddenly took him from out of nowhere.

Until he paused mid-way as he then heard two people come around the corner idly chatting loudly.

Hearing them long before seeing them due to his sharp vampire hearing, which had always been his strong point. The man as he came into sight he found himself admiring from afar.

Was his recently discovered bisexuality coming out to play again?

No, it was more about the impressive tats there etched on the bloke, unlike nothing that he had seen before all over the man's skin. Deacon had made his mind so that it could not look at another as anything more than simply just a passing interest.

Fess found though that he wasn't sad about this as much as he thought that he would be. After all, he could hardly lay claim to the delicious auburn-haired beauty of his and then go off stalking others for a quick feel, could he?

It was a one-man vs one-man relationship that he wanted.

Talking to a smaller curvy redhead beside him, the muscled guy with just as many tats as she spoke roughly.

"Thanks for letting me come with, Vi." Mr Tat smiled sincerely to his companion as Fess watched like an invisible peeping Tom.

 A softie hidden under that harder shell.

It made Fess think of his own few mates back there in the hidden realms whom he had not seen since his great escape from being turned into a living fire ball.

The realms - ones kept out of the sight of human eyes.

Did they miss him?

Had they even noticed that he was not up there with him?

Things had been eerily quiet he had found to his dismay, also slight relief.

Too quiet.

The stranger's rogue-like nature evident for Fess to see for he possessed his own devilishly rogue ness, who also nearly didn't move out of the way in time for he was that invested in the two strangers wittering conversation with each other.

The lady held a rat-like dog in her arms.

Brown. Fluffy. Mangily.

Fess found them both refreshing. His kind of folks - that were until he heard the name - Deacon. He let out a fierce growl that caused the lady to gasp when she heard a growl from out of nowhere.

Nearly dropping her beloved dog who also yelped.

"What the fucking hell was that!" The woman said shuddering openly and clutching her ratty-appearing dog tightly so that they didn't slip her grasp.

The dog stared right at Fess with bulging eyes. Animals he found could often see him when humans for sure couldn't. This one could as it started to yip and try to bite him as it passed.

Fucking thing! Cheeky fuck!

The man sighed, "I don't know. Let's go inside so I can bump into him again. Act normal Vi. Please, sis. I beg of you!"

Sis? Interesting…

Waggling her brows, "Me! Normal. Purlease…you are the one who has the crush and is stalking me to the vets." She teased as sisters like to do.

Fess clenched his fists and gritted his teeth in anger at this. The man was one step closer to signing his own death warrant and he didn't even know it yet, but he decided he would be lenient as it appeared the handsome male knew his Deacon quite well.

Should he care?

Oh, he did.

Maybe Deacon should get a tat. Property of Fess in big, bold letters. Mmm...

As the crushing human played with his smartphone to and gazed at his man's number, yes, his man! Fess was tempted to stick the man's phone politely where the sun didn't shine. But he didn't as he gathered that the man would likely enjoy it if he did so.

Seeming the type.

So, instead of this, he reached out and sticking a well-timed leg out tripping the guy over. Enjoying his fall just as much as the homophobic irate man from earlier, if not more, as the woman nearly dropped her dog. Again.

He would apologise for nothing - they both deserved everything that came their way.

Fess knew that he outshone that mere man, that walking flesh, a million times over plus one. His wit, charm, his looks, were up there with the best of them. He only had one flaw that he knew of except the awful marks, that he could not offer his man that some other knight in twatting armour may, was that – he could not be seen.

Later

Deacon left his place of work and waved goodbye to Abi
after seeing her to her nearby pink car. He glanced around to
make sure that a certain blonde-haired male was not about to
jump out of the shadows at him, pin him down and bite him
– one could only hope.

Nope. He seemed to be all alone. Not knowing how to feel
about this.

So instead, he started his walk to his rundown home through
the busy city, needing a shower, some food and ... him.

A little while later as he was stopping - staring into a shop
window full of men's clothes, he didn't keep up with the
latest trends but liked to look nice, he stopped dead in his
tracks and sighed deeply.

There was no reflection behind him. Did vampires even have
reflections?

He guessed not as he could not see him there behind him
through the glass as he eyed the red tracksuit that would be
perfect for the gym. The only thing there was cars, buses and
people rushing home after a hard day at work and school.

Or an easy one.

He could feel him though. A pull at his soul that begged for it to be near the other. Even if he annoyed him.

But oh, that B.J.… damn!

"I know you are there Fess." He said.

Nothing.

"Fess!" An annoyed hiss from an annoyed human who was nearly frothing.

"Spoilsport."

With a sharp growl that surprised him, Fess came up slowly behind the bewildered human and once he was sure that there was no one around, he guided him to the nearby alley. Conveniently the same one as where they had first met back when.

Deacon had never thought that he would have a favourite alley way – he did now.

This one where it had all began.

Fess with a thirst like nothing else grabbed his mate by the neck with a hand. He pushed his startled, but enjoying it by the bulge jutting out of his trousers, man to the wall with a passionate groan.

Groping him, kissing him roughly in possession so hard that Deacon squealed.

"Mine! You are fucking mine, do you hear me?" Fess stopped the kiss and jabbed a clawed finger into the man who was now his.

Drawing it down his neck. Licking the blood drop that leaked from it.

"You, you said we were just mates. You need to make your mind up." Deacon stammered defiantly.

Fess sniffed the neck that enticed him so very much, especially now that he smelled blood as his human adorably stammered in his nervousness.

His favourite place to smell - on his favourite person. Not that Fess liked many people. All ties to humans had been severed when his humanity had.

Until now...

Fess grinned after a final lick to the neck, "I will explain when we get in what this truly means my impatient Deacon. It is a bit much of a conversation to have here on the street. Here, I nicked these for you, so people don't think you are a loon when you talk to me." Handing his human some bright green headphones.

Obviously stolen. Designed for a teen.

"Thank you." Deacon pulled away with a pleased smile as he glanced at the shiny, bright headphones – popping them on. Adjusting his auburn hair.

Sometimes it felt so right with Fess, that he almost forgot that only he could see him!

Fess growled.

Not liking the distance between them and tried to pull his auburn-haired one closer to no avail who was just not having it.

Who pushed back again.

What the! Fess was narked. Really narked.

Deacon slapped his hand, "Let us go home. And oh, I know what you did to my dad. And to Stevie. We will be having words, you, and I!" Now it was Deacons' turn to jab. "Stevie."

A growl at the mention of another man's name. Especially that one! One who could give Fess a run for his money and who was human to go with it! Who didn't need to rely on blood to live. To not go mad in blood lust.

"Yes, Stevie. You will explain what you did when we get home."

"Fine." Fess spat and grabbed his mate's smaller warm hand and took it with his own one, rubbing it and then slipping it in to is.

He had never held hands with anyone before, shown affection to them before, but he found – he wanted to.

It felt…nice.

Warm. Cosy.

The contrast of warm human skin to his cool vampire skin felt strange, but it was certainly agreeable.

No, that was not it either. The reason that he liked it, liked this blushing man.

It felt…normal.

He felt sickeningly happy that he could forget that he had died, been tortured, burned, forget that he had been banished - twice.

All he wanted was this destiny. He wanted - Him.

This place, this rotten alley, would be etched on his cold, dead heart for all eternity.

They eventually after making stuttered small talk amongst flirtatious glances got into the dusky flat and Deacon slammed the door to. Ignoring Fess`s' grimacing at the tattered door.

He might like perfection – yes, he was messy at home though his clothes were not, but he liked the area, and it was a short distance from work, the gym, and other things that he needed.

He didn't have the time to clean.

Placing his stuff down in the corner out of the way and ripping the headphones clean off.

For someone who liked perfection, Fess found that his human was certainly a messy old fucker! You wouldn't think it by looking at him.

"Oh, you cleaned!" Deacon exclaimed with joyful surprise as he looked back and forth between the vampire and his newly tidy home. One that had not looked that way in a long time. "Thank you!"

Possibly wondering silently if the vampire had hired a cleaner…

"Maybe…" Now it was Fess`s turn to blush. Loving the whole pleasing his mate thing.

"Well, if you didn't then I have had a cleaning burglar who was frankly useless as nothing seems to have been taken!" Deacon teased.

"Trust me D, no one would burgle this flat and live to tell the tale. I would kill them flat out." A hint of a warning beneath the snarling words.

"I suppose that is one thing you are good for!"

"One thing…" A predatory look.

Remembering with a lust-filled gaze the encounter in the small veterinary office, staff room.

Where not only the animals got fantastic service.

"You know that was good…" An awkward side shuffle and Fess's favourite cheek blushing from blatant teasing by the scorched vampire.

A raise of the dark blonde brows, "Just good?"

"Fantastic then."

"Excellent." In his Mr specialised burns voice.

Deacon seemed surprised, "Oh, you watch the Simpsons? Do you get TV where you are from then? Do vampires even watch telly?" This perked his interest.

"No, we don't," Fess said in his saddest but teasing voice.

"Oh." Insert sad face.

"I am teasing you! How naïve my human is," Tutting. "We get T.V, Wi-Fi, cable. All sorts. Money is not a thing there either… we work for divine beings, so of course we would get the best things in life. Or death." Fess shrugged, "But…I

187

messed it all up and now I am stuck here in the human world. A world not meant for me." Grimacing.

Deacon appeared disappointed by this. A flicker of worry appeared over his tired face as he obviously thought the worst from hearing the vampire`s speech, "You don't want to stay?"

"I didn't..."

"But you do now?" Deacon said in a whispered hush. Hope right there in his soul. Heat in his gaze.

The intensity ran riot.

"I am never leaving you, D." Fess came up closely behind him and nibbled his neck with his teeth. The fangs could wait for later. He didn't need them.

"Because you want my blood? Is that all I am to you? A walking blood sack?" Deacon`s lip jutted out in sheer anger as he steadied himself against the wall.

This went down like a lead balloon.

The snarl to end all snarls, "What? No! I want you, Deacon. The only man that I have ever wanted. Will want. I want you until the end of time."

"Oh, Fess." Deacon turned around with a smile, letting go of the wall. His eyes almost glowing all though they wouldn't – he was only human after all.

The vampire could do enough supernatural shit for the both of them.

Fess kissed him on the cheek feeling endeared, holding the warm cheeks in his hands. The hint of a blush. His favourite thing.

It was time for the truth to come out.

Fess began, he was the one now that was nervous, "Deacon, if I am honest with you, I used to have blood multiple times a day when I was a soul collector. Now I have it every morning, from you, and it is still not enough for me. I am recovering from multiple injuries, my burns, scars, and damaged wings as you know, so I need even more than usual." He frowned, "But I manage it for you. Don't think I don't do anything by you. I will stay here in this…flat for you. I don't feed off other people for you."

A gasp.

"I did not know Fess. I really didn't. Did you want more?" A wrist was offered. An offer of substance. The offer was quickly denied.

"Yes, I do want more. More of you, the blood can wait!" pushing the wrist away even though it was filled with temptation.

189

"Aw." They kissed and Deacon whimpered needily. Then he had an idea, "Listen Vamp." Mind racing.

"Hmm?"

"You know what you said earlier bout bad guys? I do not feel comfortable offering my neck up to you more than once a day, maybe two. Hang on let me finish," He said as Fess scowled at him, but not from the lack of food, "So what I mean is you could bite some bad people? Take their blood? As long as you don't kill them... and you get the substance you so needed from them..."

Excitement rose, "You sure?"

"Yes. As long as you don't go for any man that you find attractive."

"You do know that I am clearly bi here, D? What about the woman out there?" Fess laughed.

And there was the look of disappointment from the dark-haired blusher again, "Oh. So, this might thing between us may not last-"

"Oh, don't you even finish that sentence human!" Fess growled and clenched his claws, fangs, and anything else that he could clench together.

Oh, he clenched all right!

Deacon grew wide-eyed at his angry, hot vamp. Sure, he was about to blow a fuse and he might get caught in the crossfire. If that happened then it could be a week's supply of blood all at once for the angry vamp…

A snap, "We need to talk. And you said you wanted to talk about Daddy."

Deacon wrinkled his nose," Ew. Don't call him that."

"No, that would be me." A smirk and a hint of red eyes. Passion. Wanting.

Temptation was at the door. Would he answer it?

Now was not the time to.

  Deacon chuckled back dirtily.

Breaking the tension that would either involve clothes ripping or even maybe fists swinging, he went off to make them both hot drinks, being a good host this time, himself a coffee and Fess wanted a builders cup of tea with a side order of bourbon biscuits.

Fat chance of there being any in that building…

Did he want it in a dainty cup? He assumed the vamp would be more of a beer man.

Or blood…

 He clearly needed the beer though as he sat down on his creamy sofa. Fess sat down next to him. Legs touching. Fess started to footsie him. Running his long leg up and down Deacon's twitching thigh.

Naughty.

"Oh god." The vampire smirked evilly, "You smell simply delicious." Fangs twitching.

Deacon rolled his eyes, "Let's chat then now we are seated. Don't try and change the subject now. You can have some blood later if you be honest with me now." A waggling warning finger. "You know what you did when I was on the way to work. Good looks do not let you get away with anything you please! My mum rang and oh my that was an awkward conversation. She is irritating at the best of times!"

"Yes, cos everyone can see my good looks!"

A sore point obviously for Fess. For who wanted to be unseen?

Maybe someone with social anxiety. No one else.

"Sorry. But still…"

Fess moved closer, "Look. I am not the bad guy here, D. Your dad was spouting shit to your neighbour about you, so I pushed him over in retaliation for it. Ask her. That Stevie." He spat, "Was boasting to his sister about his bloody crush on you. Fucking hell! Tripping him up? Yes, yes, I did. He is lucky that I didn't push him in front of a nearby truck going

192

at full speed with the brakes cut. The perks of being unseen dear human. No one, but no one, would have suspected me." A boastful grin at this.

"Ok..." Deacon began to look doubtful at this. "Maybe you should go now..." Clutching his chest with a hand at how deep he was getting into.

One that still beat.

"Go. Where the fuck am I supposed to go?" A sarcastic laugh from a fang-filled mouth.

A sadistic one.

One that was clearly never leaving this human alone as long as he lived. Not even a burning had kept him away.

Decapitation – maybe, although he would still likely try...

"I am out of my depth here, Fess. I cannot have you putting people that I care about in danger. Or me. My dad used to beat me, and he threw me out for being gay like it was the eighteenth century...my mother she -" A sad smile.

"He bloody what?" Red lined Fess`s vision, fangs bit through his swollen mouth. Purple blood spilt down his furious mouth.

Again. He had anger issues. Deacon issues.

Deacon paced the room nervously, "I do not want him back in my life. Or my ma and we only talk on the phone now. I do not know why he turned up. But that is for me to decide and me alone about whether I see him. Not you, not my friends, not anyone!" He yelled getting angry.

That soon shut the vampire up.

Fess looked at him with a new sense of admiration for this outburst. Surely the almighty and powerful vampire should be the one to take care of his weak ass, fragile human? For he was the one who held the power, the immortality.

The invisibility?

But he had a funny feeling now that Deacon had it all handled. He had had to given his useless parents sadly.

Fess had a feeling that if he pushed him then he could drive his mate away and he didn't want that! He needed him. Wanted him...couldn't survive an eternity without him...

Fess waved his hands in gesture, "Fine...fine." A defeated sigh. "But he beat you up? He was lucky he didn't get buried under the patio then."

"I don't have a patio." Deacon smiled and sipped his coffee. Wincing at how hot it was.

"Ok, ok, so I get it. No interfering." A nod.

"No interfering."

"Ok, my little mate."

"And not so much of the little." He casually slapped Fess`s arm who growled at impact. Deacon looked startled and shot up out of the way, off the sofa, almost losing his coffee in the process.

"Deacon…" Stern red tinged eyes looked his way.

Regrettable ones.

"Yes…?" He replied nervously.

Now fidgeting.

Fess looked him straight in the eyes. Eyes a deep river of red, but kind, "I would never hurt you. Only in the bedroom though. You know that right?" He grunted.

A sigh.

"Deacon?" Fess repeated.

"Yes."

"I would rather end my own immortal life than to ever hurt a hair of your pretty, well-groomed auburn head. Understand?"

"I think so. It is not that I thought you would hurt me, you made me jump. I just hate being called little by anyone, Fess. Stevie calls me little whenever I see him for some reason or another. When I was at school I was taken the piss of for being small, spotty, and overweight and because I had auburn hair. You know what it is like when you are at school. People pick on anything and everything. I had a growth spurt and then lost the weight..." He rushed, placing his cup down and sitting back down next to the undead one.

"A growth spurt? You can say that!" Hungry eyes admiring the other one's crotch that the more he looked at it the more it noticeably jutted out.

"Fess!"

"Well, I like everything about you." Fess ran a hand lightly up Deacon's body while running his fingers through his lovely hair. Stopping as he reached an upper thigh. Keeping his hand there.

In ownership.

But Deacon did not know it yet. Oh, he would!

"You Are hardly little." A roll of the eyes. "You are a similar build to me." Fess said.

"I was. I like everything about you too."

"Except for my scars!" Fess hissed.

Oh. Them.

"Yes, to start with I admit I was startled by them. When we first met I was overtaken by your handsomeness, Fess. Your whole demeanour."

Fess smiled still looking unsure.

Deacon continued, "And to see you like that... it did make me uncomfortable. I strive for perfection. Except my housework of course!" He gestured around, "But now, when I look at you, look at them...all I feel is hatred for the one who caused them in the first place. If I could see them, this Rhys - which I assume I couldn't, then I would have a million dark thoughts of my own. As you do. I feel the same way."

Deacon touched the cool face of the startled immortal in his flat who looked to be lost for words at that place in time.

He went to get up - "Now, I am going to get the lube and you are going to show me how much like mates we are not as you take me to pound town."

"Pound town!" An amused laugh by the fanged one.

Deacon walked quickly to his bedroom as if his ass was burning, which it soon would be, and hastily grabbed the lube, racing back to Fess who was waiting eagerly. Now stripped of everything. Stroking himself...hard.

"Oh, wow!"

Deacon also stripped with as much eagerness now and grabbing the stronger one began to passionately kiss his vamp who growled with passion, as their lips locked together in tandem.

Their tongues touched. Feeling each other, no, pawing each other frantically with lust, Fess guided his naked man, his naked Deacon, until he was bent over the sofa waiting for what was coming to him.

Waiting for Fess to lube his pretty arsehole. To feed him his awaiting cock in it which was made for it.

"I want to eat your ass first."

The vampire licked his lips hungrily eying the sweet butt cheeks with the target in the middle.

"Oh!" But Deacon should have known how quick in his haste Fess would be as he was with anything that took his fancy. And Deacon took his fancy.

For no sooner had he muttered oh, than there was a tongue flickering into his awaiting hole. Lapping it up.

Vampires had super speed after all...

"Oh my god! And another thing that you haven't done I am guessing, but you are a pro at." Deacon squeezed his eyes shut tight in his arse eaten bliss.

"Shut up and take my rimming, my annoying human!" The sound of a quick spank to the bum and a sharp crying out.

"Fucking bossy! Aren't you? Oh – oh, my god!" Deacon squirmed beneath the mouth that lingered on his arsehole and the tongue that was now exploring his insides like a slithering snake.

Deacon was that close to coming from that alone until the thick-lipped mouth was urgently replaced by a nuzzling cock again.

Nudging his warm awaiting entrance.

"No actually-" Fess said as he flipped the groaning, panting male over and carried him straight to the bedroom as if he was a well-endowed firefighter in a previous life.

"Woah!"

Marvelling obviously at how strong the vamp was.

Fess laid Deacon down gently. As if he wouldn't dare to hurt a hair on his head. When actually he had the power to do what he pleased – to get away with it.

To kill him.

And Deacon seemed excited by that. He knew he wouldn't, but the thought was there!

"I want to watch you come this time," Fess confessed licking his lips.

"Ok…wait… wow!"

A nod as the cock was back nudging the wet entrance again. Then with the help of a little lube – pushed into Deacon's tight entrance with a gasp.

They both started groaning.

Fess could feel every tight thrust right into his man as he ramped it up a notch – or ten of them. Starting off gently so as not to hurt him, and then taking them both higher and higher – who needed wings for this?

He didn't.

He got them out anyway, glorious black ones for only his human to see, as his pleasure took him, took them, higher and higher. Coming off the ground a bit which was all that he could do.

As Fess thrust eagerly into his dripping, sweaty human, the one even though his own heart was still, he could feel himself falling in love with – not just lust – more. He could feel the tight hole around his cock and just wanted to burst so fucking badly. Jesus!

Deacon

Deacon looked at the monster like vampire pounding into him hard on the bed, his bed, as if he would never have sex again and had to make the most of it because that was the end.

As if he wanted to own him in every way. Oh, that he did already…Fess had owned him since that evening there in the stinking alleyway. When he had at first heard a woman screaming and found heaven itself, his vampire instead.

He should be scared by this whole thing; he should run away kicking and screaming and get as far away as was possible if he could do. But this here vamp could own him.

Just as he felt he owned him back in return. They might be different in certain ways from each other. Deacon a sensitive man, whilst Fess did not have a sensitive bone in his body. Or did he?

Maybe he did except that it was only the eager human who saw that side of him that was buried away deep from others searching gazes.

For Fess had been banished from his home – twice and forced to hang around with a nutter older vamp for nearly ten years. This Rhys.

But somehow even still - they just…fit.

The cock, thick and long, longer than his normal human-sized one was having no mercy on his quivering body.

Shaking with his desire for the unnatural one, Deacon could feel the monstrous, bigger blonde male, but still beautiful – scars and all he guessed, about to finish in him as he gripped him tighter. "I am going to come, Fess. Jeez!" He gasped as the waves got ready to hit him full force.

When they hit they would embrace him!

"Me too," Fess grunted.

But before the nearly shuddering vamp did, he slowed right down and took hold of the trembling humans hands with his own ones and said with his cock still inside, "When I said mates Deacon, I didn't mean fucking friends, that would never do - I meant fated mates. Destiny. Vampires have a fated human mate and you it turns out are my one. Mine to keep. I am going to come in that dirty hole of yours and in the morning taking that mouth with it. Filling you up in every way possible - You are mine, as I am yours for all of fucking eternity and beyond it!"

And with this, they both came hard together in a sea of fluids. Tears in their eyes - still hand in hand as the vampire's almighty cock finally came to a juddering stop at its destination. Deacon followed shortly after that, taking his cock in hand with the vampire's cock shoved deep in place. He would remember this day until the day that he died. Hopefully not yet.

But one day in the future.

The day that he found out what that strange, intense pull was between them. The one that locked them in and would never let them go. The one that was destiny – and destiny didn't wait for no one.

Would one day he have to become a vampire also, he wondered? To be with his mate. He could not bear to be apart from him.

Scars and all. Every single inch.

"Lay down." Deacon was urged as Fess pulled his dripping cock away and got ready to stand up to clean up.

Seeking his clothes in a flurry.

"No, come here." Deacon now grabbed the naked vampire with the svelte butt and pulled him in for a sweet loving lingering kiss that made them both tremble. Then he ran his hands up and down Fess`s torso. Feeling each and every part of the exposed skin which he tried to hide.

Bringing lips lovingly down to kiss the vampire`s scars one by one.

Ones that the vamp didn't deserve to receive even though he knew that he felt that he did. Deacon liked perfection – but he liked Fess more.

Much more. He adored him. In every way.

If he could rip those scars away from that pale, breathless body and put them onto his own one - he would. Even if it would make him feel the way that he used to feel, ugly – he would.

Unfortunately, he couldn't, the scars would have to stay.

"You don't have to do this." Fess murmured.

"I want to. I love every part of you, and I am sorry that I made you feel otherwise." Deacon whispered afterwards. Affection and understanding deep in his gaze as Fess eyed him like he was the best thing to happen to him in all of his lifetime.

Because he was.

Then they lay in each other's arms - to just forget the world.

CHAPTER TEN

A few blissful months later

Deacon

"I have a surprise for you, my sexy D." The blonde and naughty vamp said after they panted after a hot, sweaty session. Lying in bed together curled up as one, Fess spooning his man possessively as he liked to do – wings spread out as his man liked them to be, running his claws up and down the blushing man, the filled man, the other enjoying the sensation of danger that those claws held in them.

 The usual for them now - night after night.

Day after day - which it was now.

Soon, Deacon would have to go to work, so he was making the most of having his cock obsessed vamp by his side - or right there at his back.

After a shuddering start, Fess had gotten the place looking like he wanted it- habitable, clean, theirs. Choosing to stay there whilst his little vet nurse did his job each week day. Weekends were just for them.

No one would come between their Friday popcorn and movie night. Vampire version of - Netflix and chill.

Not going out much, not wanting to bump into Rhys or anyone who could tell him where he was.

Who might see his human. He couldn't bear it.

"Ohhh, what is it?" Deacon nuzzled back towards him.

Moaning at the bite at his neck where the fangs teased. Tempted to stick right in and take a bite of their victim.

Enjoying the wetness, the smell of sex that lingered still on his thighs as it dripped from his used hole.

They had gotten into a routine of Fess being in charge in the bedroom – and that was how he liked it.

Deacon also.

The vamp on top and him taking it hard, loving it, wanting it more and more each day as their bond ravelled all the more tighter together. Being ravished whilst the other was in vampire mode.

Winged, fanged, clawed, for only him to see.

Craving the undead one so fucking bad – wishing that he had died instead of him.

After all, whilst Deacon`s own parents were low-life's, Fess had told him how close he was to his own family before he had died.

How he had been forced to be separated from them, never to see them again – only the once. To say his silent goodbye.

Fess winked naughtily and swung around on the bed.

Their bed.

Patting the chequered duvet.

"That would be telling. Meet me after work pronto and be prepared as you are about to meet another vampire. Well.. kinda meet." A shrug.

As Deacon wouldn't see them.

Fess had nearly bitten his neck off when the curious Deacon had asked whether he may see another vamp, saying that was reserved for mates and mates only. Deacon still struggled to understand the whole invisible vampire thing. How one could see them when others could not? It did not make sense.

It was surreal.

"Oh." So then also got out and went to seek his work things. Still not very organised. Still messy.

"Deacon? My lit… lively human?"

"Lively?" Eyes narrowed at the near little slip up.

"Well, you are alive, are you not?" Fess came up behind him still naked, scars showing in all of their brazen beauty. Ones that now Deacon didn't take much notice to.

He saw the vamp behind the scars. His man.

"I can smell the blood pumping through your –"

"Fess…" A groan, "Yes, I am alive. Everything is alive now," giggling. Nodding to his cock which had sprung to life again. "I am trying to get ready."

The vampire nodded appreciatively, "That is good as I have no air to resurrect you sadly. It would kill me – again, if anything happened to you my blushing Deacon. I want to keep you by my side forever, keep you safe. If I did not know how much you loved your work then I would lock your door, throw away the key and be done with it!"

That sounded good.

Moving away - throwing his uniform on with haste and ignoring the bristling jealousy that shot uncharacteristically through him as the smitten Deacon thought about Fess meeting another vampire.

His own kind. He was only human. Nothing special after all…

"You would do my head in." He smiled with affection.

"Which one?" A blonde tilt of the head.

"Both."

A chuckle, "What troubles you?" Fess was obviously smarter than he looked. He might be blonde, but he didn't miss anything. He was certainly not stupid.

"Deacon…" He began frowning.

A sigh, "I worry that if you see another vampire then you will fly off with them into the sunset. Leave me here."

"On these wings?" Flicking the dark crooked wings back into his body with a groan as it hurt, Fess frowned as he felt the worry ooze off his mate, "She is just my exes sister. We always got on better than me and my ex did. I saw her and we had a chat."

"Peachy."

"Oh, my own mortal is jealous." Fess stalked over with a manic grin, his sights on his anxious human, "She has no interest in me. She has a mate - a woman. A human one. I

shall introduce you at some point all though Ruby is as
possessive of her pretty Imogen as I am -"

"Imogen… I know an Imogen. Works near me. Blonde, tall,
lean-"

"Quirky." Fess finished, "Yes, that is her. Ruby is now also
earth residing and Imogen's friends have helped them to set
up home, and what not. She, after slapping me for
kidnapping her sister agreed to help."

"Surprised she did to be fair."

"Me too. You see, Vampires have longer lives than humans
do, and so grudges do not stick around for as long as. Now
stop with the silly jealousy and go to work my chaotic
human. If you are not outside your work at five sharpish
then I will come inside it and take possession of you in every
wicked way."

"I will be."

"Good boy."

Remembering the last time that the vamp had stalked him at
work causing mischief and mayhem which only he could see
and so now Deacon had banned a displeased Fess from there
unless it was a true emergency. "See you then!" Giving the
blonde that made him swoon a kiss on the cheek, which

nearly ended up in a passionate embrace again as he was pawed not subtly.

"Sure, you don't want me to walk you?" Fess said making toast and tea. Although the fridge was now stocked with more appetising foods that he wanted to eat.

"No, I'm good."

"Be safe, D." A caring, hushed whisper.

"I will try."

Later

Fess grabbed Deacon's hand as soon as he tiredly left the veterinary practice and dragged him two streets away by his arm. He seemed to be in a rush to get somewhere.

Not explaining where. Just directing.

"Where are we going?" A laughing Deacon said.

"Here." They stopped mid-step.

Huh?

"I'm confused," Deacon said. What were they supposed to be looking at?

"That!" Fess pointed next to them.

"It's a car. A sports car. Not sure what make that is as that is more your thing. It's lovely. What of it? I know you like cars, ok, love cars, but…"

It was a red sports car with shiny paintwork that gleamed in the late afternoon sun.

A pleased grin, "That is a Porsche. It's yours."

"A Porsche! Wow… mine? Where did it come from? Did you steal it?" Narrowed eyes pointed the vampires away in accusation. Expecting for the alarm to go off on the car any minute now and the owner to come running and screaming. Deacon had had words with the vampire after he had stolen a few things here and there.

Begged him not to do it again.

 What with being a good member of the community.

Fess clearly hadn't gotten the memo.

But he explained, "Ruby couldn't make it, something came up. She helped me access my money, D. Her Imogen's, human friends did. This is yours and I have brought you a home. Us a home," Fess clutched his mates startled hand with a tear in his eye as the emotion poured through. "You said you have a license yeah? Now get in!" He laughed as Deacon stood there speechless with a mouth like a fish, then shrugging, taking the keys, hopped right into the driver's seat like a pro.

Fess sidled in next to him, possessive hand on knee.

"I don't know what to say..." Deacon began. Glancing around the gorgeous car. One that he would never be able to afford.

Overcome with emotion right then.

His vampire, his Fess had brought him a car? A home for them?

It was all too much. Way too much.

No body, but nobody, no human, had ever treated Deacon as well as his vampire had ever had.

His imperfect – perfect for him - vamp.

Radio on high, lady Gaga blaring, window down, they set off.

"Can we drive to the coast first?" Deacon asked.

"Lets. It`s your car, drive where you bloody want!"

So, he did.

A short half an hour later, Deacon pulled up at the still sunny coast in a deserted spot and cut the engine.

"So, what do you think?" Red eyes blared in the early evening sun at their intended target. Loving the car. Loving the man.

"You not going to melt, vamp?" Deacon teased.

"Only for you." Fess tutted, "Heck, that was cheesy!" Pretending to barf.

"I know," Leaning over to kiss him, "Thank you Fess."

"Deacon, it should be me thanking you. At first I admit that I was surprised that I was mated to a man. You have given me everything that I could wish for plus so much more. I love that blush, that grateful smile. The proudness in your work, the groan as you –"

"Fess!" And there was said blush.

"I have a way you can thank me!" Gesturing at his now proud boner making the vampire`s black trousers have a tent in.

"You didn't have to buy me an expensive car to get me to suck you off, Fess! I would do that any way! I enjoy it."

And Deacon got to work once the vampires cock was sprung free from its restraints.

The surrounding skin was pale and cool, the cock was still human so like that you would not know that Fess was anything but human, whilst his fangs, claws and eyes remained in check.

Deacon opened his mouth and took it all in, Fess gently pushed his man's head down as he let the seat down slight to get a better position. An expert at it, one hand gripped the end while his mouth worked his shuffling mate into oblivion. As he neared filling his mates mouth -

"Stop. That is enough. Rub your cock against mine now, D. We will come together."

An order.

Deacon did not have to think twice about this. Taking his own aroused one out of his trousers and then gently rubbing it fully erect up and down, Fess`s own glorious length.

"Your cock is made for me! You are made for me!" A groan as Deacon took them both in hand with the dominating vampire under him. Rubbing them both together, making it work, and then jerking them both off vigorously.

"Yes, yes, I am!"

For he was. He really was.

Not long after this as they both reached their peak and came in a sea of liquids and fierce yells they drove off.

To their new home.

The vampire and his human mate.

As one.

EPILOGUE

Fess scowled as his mate got ready to go to the local pub nearby.

Without him. What a bloody cheek! Who would have thought it? The nerve!

He had been going every Friday as of late after work and the gym, and after Fess had kicked off the first time that it had happened since he had been asked to stay with his mate there in his grubby flat, now not so grubby, Fess had realised that he was the one who would occasionally have to bow down and take it like a man - and not in the bedroom that were. Because Deacon wasn't budging on that.

He was his own man, made his own rules and did his own thing.

As long as he whispered sweet nothings into his vampire's ear then who was he to grumble?

The house at the edge of the city that they had drove to that day was amazing. Four bedrooms, lots of rooms and a garden with summer house for over 18 vamp and human fun. A large garage with room for cars for fess to tinker with. Soon they would be moving into it once they had packed up their things there.

Not that Fess had many things to pack. But he was getting there, slowly, but surely.

The thing that had made Deacon openly weep, wasn't the car, the house, garden, or the picket white fence. Or the sweet I love you from Fess as he took in Deacon's happy smile that things were turning out more amazing then he could have ever hoped.

It was the large, spacious annex at the side of the house, for when Deacon became a qualified vet at long last in the next few years.

His own practise.

No one had ever done anything as adorable as that. He could not wait to make the place their home.

Their home!

"Are you sure you are ok with me going?" Deacon asked sweetly as he prepped his hair, making it perfect, in the bathroom's full-length mirror. Not seeming to be able to get the tuft of hair at the front right.

But Fess, as his eyes crinkled in amusement at his man in the mirror knew that his little firecracker with the auburn hair, may say that right then as he got himself ready to go out to meet the guys, but by lord he knew that he was going anyway no matter what the grumpy immortal said or did!

"Not really."

The vamp shuffled his feet awkwardly and plonked down onto the sofa with a pretend huff.

Avoiding eye contact. Showing that he was sulking about the pub going.

"You could come with?" Deacon paused in the mirror briefly and looked hopefully at Fess now sprawled on the sofa drinking beer, remote in the other. It seemed that he was a beer man after all...

And blood.

Once a day usually when he was taking his mate hard up the ass, he took a sup of Deacon's delicious neck also - right at the peak.

Deacon had actually found that he liked it after a while of feeling unsure about being a walking, talking, human drink. The thought of Fess going hungry made him shudder though as did him drinking off another...

Fess crunched the beer can in his hand now finished and rolled his eyes to the sky. Deacon didn't mind the beer drinking as Fess was a godsend at cleaning up he had discovered, and it gave him something to do besides to try to keep him away from anyone with a dick.

Kept him out of mischief and he certainly liked that...

Imagining the vamp naked with a pinny on.

Who would have ever thought that the once fiery vampire who liked all eyes on him would become domesticated and a step away from love...?

And he didn't mind it!

He didn't care that he was mated to a man now when he had at first or gave a shit about what anyone would think about it.

Love would do that to a guy...

Gone were the days of impressing anyone. Fess just wanted to impress Deacon, he craved him, but he knew he did not need to, for he had his beating heart anyway all the way.

"No, there is something I need to do."

Fess became serious.

"Oh?" Deacon raised an enquiring brow.

Looking worried by this.

"You know I said about Barren and the blood farm? And his mate maybe being there?"

"Yes…" Deacon's lip turned up in displeasure.

This very topic straight after Fess having confided in him about turning all those poor, defenceless women into vampires and some ending up dead as he at first had gotten the whole turning somebody thing wrong… that had been the cause of the first proper argument between them.

One that ended in them thankfully ripping their clothes off later and you know…

Fess looked the shorter male square in the eyes and said, "It is time to make amends D. You taught me that. Barren deserves it, he was good to me before I went off the rails."

An agreeing nod in return.

Deacon would have his back either way whether he agreed with it or not. After all wasn't compromise something that couples sometimes had to do?

Fess begrudgingly got up, "I will walk my hot and sexy man to the pub with all thought on licking him from head to toe and then try and find Barren. Help him."

He had not told him that he had seen Barren about in the city more than once, ok a lot. And frankly – that he had looked like shit. The thought of his own man, his D, being taken and

221

never returned filled Fess with an utmost rage where he could burn everyone and everything, to the ground! He would burn again just like he had before in order to protect his mate from harm's way!

"You know it wasn't your fault, right?" The human whispered sweetly. Body thrumming.

"No, but I could have helped."

"Did he help you when you were injured and lying on the ground?" A bite of anger with these mere words.

"No."

Deacon waved his hands angrily, "You be nice, you get treated nice."

"Oh, I will remember that!" Fess came up and nibbled his stubble along Deacon's neck, who definitely stopped what he was doing!

A small whimper left his lips. "I might be extra nice..." An honorary growl.

"Oh...I might forget the pub if you carry on Fess." A deep smile that made the sullen one smile too.

A growl of possession, "You think? Say my name again. I like it on your lips."

"Fess. Oh fuck!" A nibble at the neck. Then Fess teased him by stopping it altogether. Damn it!

"Not now, my mortal." Fess scolded his needy human. Yes, his. "I nearly said little. Enjoy the pub and think of me ploughing my cock in your ass, but not before you give me one of those oh, so delicious blow jobs that you are so good at."

A giggle and a firm nod. "Deal."

"You behave."

"As always."

"Is Stevie going then…?" A warning bite.

Stevie had been cropping up more and more as of late and they both knew that it was time for him to be told that the object of his crush was now eternally attached.

Forever.

By a bond that not even he could break.

For even if no other human could see Fess, Deacon always would.

"You know he is. I told you this earlier in the week. I want to introduce him to my new friend Ru. Remember the one who came to see in the alley when you were busy kidnapping an innocent woman? I did not realise that he is gay also and I think they will really hit it off. Ru has that whole sweet and sensitive thing going on that Stevie likes."

"Pah! You are hardly sweet and sensitive, although you like having me take you hard until you…"

"Fess!" A blush. Oh, he could act soft and sweet…

"And of my ex?" Fess said "She is no innocent. Elfina can more than handle herself in every way. And yes, I remember. The Australian? The interfering old busybody."

Grimacing.

Another handsome male whom the vamp wanted to keep away. And this one was actually a daddy, and not just a player like Stevie were.

"Mmm. That's the one." A shared smile. Ru and Deacon had become closer since their strange alley experience back when. Ru knew that Deacon had seen more than he had let on, but he had been gentlemanly enough not to probe him too much…

And so, hand in hand they were out the door together as one. The rogue vampire and his human.

Deacon nuzzled his dirty blonde's shoulder happily.

If he could have known what would happen next then he would have stayed at home after all…

Later

"What are you doing here, Fess?" A sigh as a usually put-together posh one Barren put down his beer bottle. Ok, more like he threw it across the way so that it nearly hit Fess in the chest. He assumed that was an accident.

A scowl on seeing the lighter-haired vamp as if he had dragged in dog shit through his newly carpeted house.

"I want to help." Fess said cautiously.

"You?" A sarcastic laugh of disbelief from the posh one.

"Yes, me."

"How?" That had piqued Barren's interest.

"Listen, I know some of Rhys`s hidden places. I might be able to find out the whereabouts of…"

"Don't say it!" A pained expression fell over Barren who grabbed another bottle from his grey-tattered bag of obviously stolen human goods.

"OK, OK!" A begrudged sigh from Fess, "As my wings are damaged and I cannot fly more than a few metres off the ground, I decided as I cannot soul call any more to take something up with the realm keepers and they gracefully accepted."

Narrowed-eyed, "Go on…"

"Barren, I am going to try to help keep the Earth-dwelling vampires in check. It seems that a few have come apart from the rest and gone on to do darker things that even astound me as of late. The realms are not happy about this. They said it has to stop!"

A Scoff, "I don't blame them. This was not what we were made for! We were made for good."

"Yes."

"I have seen you around the city with your fellow. I am glad to see that he has made you see the errors of your ways. I did not think this was possible." Barren nodded.

A look of dread filled Fess`s spine at these mere words with a bite of warning. If Barren had noticed that he was alive and had escaped the burning that had been sent his way, mated to a man, and living happy as Larry in the human world, then how long before Rhys did?"

A clock was ticking that he had no control over...

"Rhys knows." Barren said gently.

And there it was...it had happened way quicker than expected.

"I did not tell him, I swear the words did not leave my lips. I might think you are an annoying runt, but I wouldn't do that to your human. He looks nice." Barren continued, taking a glug of his beer.

"He is."

More than nice. Fess owed him the world and he would give him it on a platter.

"Good luck mate."

And before Fess could confirm anymore, Barren had flown off into the darkness. Leaving Fess with a sour taste in his mouth...

Shuddering he grabbed an unopened beer that Barren had left, opening it with his fangs he took a slow walk to the pub. He just wanted to check something out quickly...

Watching, waiting in the shadows like the predator that some used to assume him to be. Fes wondered as he watched the revellers drink their beers, smoke their fags, and have a cheeky snog with someone they shouldn't do, oh, those were the days!

But they were over in the blink of an eye.

His sudden death had seen to that. Proving that life could be there one minute and gone the next...

He wondered whether Stevie was now aware that Deacon was off limits by now. For he could hardly walk in grab his fella and say, "Hi, I am Fess, Deacon's boyfriend. Oh, and I am a vampire and if you make one more false move then I will rip your neck clean off!"

It wouldn't work in the way that he wanted it to. And if he could, he would likely drain the precious Stevie dry for daring to think he even had a chance with someone as fit as Deacon.

Oh, there he was. The tattooed ape now leaving alone - looking pissed.

Both drunk and annoyed.

Fess followed him into the dead of the night. Waiting for the perfect opportunity to strike his prey. As Stevie drunkenly stumbled as he approached a corner, no one was about, so Fess grabbed him hastily.

Claws digging in lightly to the drunk human`s massive arms, massive but he was stronger. "Leave Deacon alone. He is mine!" A growl as Fess spat into his ear.

"Where, where are you?" A slur to the drunk, bigger man's words, "Look, I don't know what the fucking hell is going on here man, but I know Deacon is spoken for. He told me just now. … so, I don't need some riff-raff trying to…"

"Oh." Fess dropped him like a sack of spuds onto the ground realising that he was acting hasty.

Deacon was going to kill him!

Stevie stumbled again unsteady on his feet and gagged, stinking of beer, so Fess propped him up again.

Probably assumed that he had had more than he thought he had to drink. That he was seeing things.

But then –

"Well, well what do we have here?" A snarl from behind them both.

Oh god. As if things couldn't get any worse. Oh, but they had…

Fess would recognise that eerie voice from behind anywhere and so he didn't even have to turn his head to have a look at the long-haired stunning ones angry face.

There would be a snarl, a pursing of the lips, red eyes to show his eternal anger.

Once it was the sound of an ally - now it was the sound of a foe. He did not dare to turn round. He did not utter a single word. He simply gazed into the stunned eyes of Stevie who could not see either of the vamps and appeared flummoxed. Fortunately.

"Are you not going to answer me then, Fess?" Rhys snapped impatiently. Used to an audience.

A bad one.

He appeared to be trying to use his dark magic yet again, Fess recognised the sound of magic in the air trying to flicker, but it appeared that the older vamp had forgotten that his magic was useless right there in the human world.

Or that it had dissolved when he bonded with his mate…

"You left me to burn." For he had. There was nothing left to say.

"It was what you deserved. The scars suit you."

"No one deserves that fate." For they didn't.

"You did…" But he didn't. Yes, he had made some mistakes. Fess, owned up to them. He would shout them from the rooftops.

Rhys, he was now slowly realising had done so much worse than he ever had over the passing years. And Rhys had had more years to make them in.

Barren was a mess as his mate had been pulled from under his feet. Justice would one day be served.

But by who?

Fess had done his time, paid his price. Rhys hadn't.

"Who is your little toy? Your mate?" Fess turned his head now feeling protective of Stevie, who was now trying to stand again.

And failing.

He was a wanker - fair. He still did not deserve to be stuck in the crossfire between those who may rip him to shreds in an instant. Deacon he knew would not have let his friend leave in this drunken, stumbling state. Vulnerable to others out there with his wallet hanging out.

Guessing that the tattooed one had snuck out of the bar before the others had noticed that he had even gone.

Fess would have to protect him though; it was all that he could do to fix this.

He was the only one who could.

But how he asked himself as the wild one scowled in displeasure. Rhys was narked and moving closer to the two-inch by-inch. Hair flying madly behind him as he gripped his leather jacket tightly. Claws digging into his own skin. Fess guessed that he liked pain.

He should know.

He could still feel it on his skin, along every burn, every scar. The ones that may fade but that would always be there.

And in his head. The memory would forever remain.

The scent of evil lingered thickly there in the air - the scent of death. How many more would die at that vampire's hands?

Before Fess could react, he was grabbed roughly by two more vampire`s whom he did not recognise, who appeared out of a gust of smoke, a goon with a bald head like a misshapen egg like humpty dumpty, and one with curly hair like a black sheep.

Slimmer than the first one.

Both as gormless as each other.

Clearly, vamps were not so fussy about who they turned these days for most vampires were beautiful, "Get off!" The blonde tried to get to Stevie in any way possible, kicking, flaying his arms, but Rhys was on him, and he hit him square in the jaw knocking his head back with a fierce crunch.

Two vamps that he knew from the darkness were holding him back while Rhys snarled in glee at the stumped nearly passed-out Stevie.

Still in the dark about what was happening right there in the street. Was he the one who was about to pay the price?

"He isn't even my mate!" Fess panicky yelled to no avail.

Fess fought the two goons as he was pushed onto the ground hard and pinned down from behind. There were too many of them, as two more skinny vamps arrived to cause havoc, and he was still recovering from his burns to have the strength to deal with it.

Deal with them all.

Deacon fed him once a day, fucking delicious, he couldn't ask for more though he needed it to return to his former glory.

Or as close as...

While his back was turned was when Rhys made his move. Sticking his fangs into Stevie who screamed and forcing Fess to try to stand up to help the frightened human- try to reach him.

His head span.

Collapsing next to the man, Rhys and his henchmen made to leave, but then – "What are you doing?" A woman's gentle voice. One he recognised.

But would she be glad to see him?

It was Justina.

Blonde silky hair, curvy and – pregnant? How could this be? Fess tried to reach Stevie with a groan on his hands and knees.

Feeling like a fool – likely looking like one.

"He killed him? Oh, my god he killed him!" Fess said as Stevie let out a gasp and then his chest stilled. Justina was now arguing with her fated mate, whilst his men flew away. Fess started chest compressions – anything that could help. Not being able to do mouth to mouth.

But he was gone.

But wait!? The sound of life if only faint.

"Get Barren, Justina."

"Did you kill him?" She snapped to Fess. Gesturing to Stevie.
Struggling to look him in the eye. She hated him. He got that.

"What, no! It was Rhys. He is still breathing. Just…"

Her head flipped round so fast as she gazed at her mate.
"Rhys?"

He murmured under his breath, "We will talk about this later
my love, you should not be here like this." Nodding at her
bump.

"Well, I am. You were acting shifty. Home. Now! I will get
Barren." She said nudging him and gripping her swollen
belly.

Fess nodded gratefully as she and her sheepish mate flew off
into the sunset together. Who would have thought that Rhys
would be under the thumb?

Mates eh!

Back to Stevie.

Fess knew deep in his unbeaten heart that there was only
one way out of this whole agonising situation as he stood
over the unconscious, possibly dead, male in disbelief. He

could not go get help and he did not know whether Stevie would even last that long for him to try.

He was barely alive as it were.

He would have to turn him. It was the only way.

If Deacon hadn't wanted to kill him earlier - he certainly would now.

Jesus wept.

"Stevie?" He whispered with tears in his eyes. He had not turned a single person since ten years ago when he was a young, arrogant vamp and had only for dubious reasons. This was life or death.

Well... kind of life. "I am sorry mate. It was my fault for being a jealous prick."

He truly was.

But back to the matter in hand.

Stevie was nearly drained of blood, so he just had to finish this. He sunk his awaiting fangs into the human, regretting having promised Deacon that he would not drink from any hot males.

He had to.

When Stevie's sweet nectar was all gone he bit into his wrist. Then he dropped some of his own blood into Stevie's mouth. And waited.

Prayed. Hoped.

And waited again. Only time would tell if he had done his duty to the still human.

His chest then went completely still. Fess froze in fright. He gently shook him.

Still nothing.

"Fess, Fess?" The sound of Deacon from nearby.

"Over here!"

He called and Deacon and Ru appeared. He had never been so glad to see Deacon in his entire life! Even if he had brought that half-wit Australian with him!

"What have you done!" Deacon cried on seeing Stevie and tried to push Fess away from Stevie's still, beatless body.

"No, no. Don't do that!" Fess urged, "I didn't do this, but I am fixing it. You two need to go. Now. Get the fuck out of here!"

"Don't you want me?" Deacon was hurt.

But then Stevie gasped, although his chest remained still.

Fess smiled anxiously, "Always. Rhys killed him, D he thought he was you. I had to turn him. You need to go. He is turning into a vampire. Please!"

"I can't see him Fess. Where has he gone?" Deacon sobbed, kneeling on the ground searching for his tattooed friend.

"He is here. He is fine." Fess stroked him.

"He is not here!"

"Who you talking to, Deacon?" Ru came over. And kneeled next to Deacon. He could obviously hear Fess and he knew after before in the alley that things in the world were more complicated than he thought.

But this was madness. Complete and utter madness.

"I can." Whispered Ru.

Not sure why he could see Deacon, but not the man whom he could hear at his side whom Deacon sounded so darn fond of. Loving even.

Again.

Or could explain why Deacon could no longer see the injured lying on the ground, a man from the pub, Stevie, whom he had been introduced to earlier there on the ground within hands reach.

A moment's touch.

Stevie's eyes opened.

A fierce scary shade of red. Red for danger.

Filled with hunger. Filled with need, and he looked right at Ru, which Fess had been surprised to learn was short for bloody Rupert, as Fess gasped in surprise that Ru although he couldn't see him could see the newly turned vamp, not before coming in the way of the oh-hungry one and his own human.

He would not put him in harm's way. He would rather burn again.

"Mine." Stevie loudly growled looking straight at Ru, right in the eyes.

And then he went right for him…

The end. For now…

Part two coming late May.

Stevie and Ru – an enemies to lovers- fated mate romance.

Printed in Great Britain
by Amazon

39910567R00138